BY BETH RAYMER

Fireworks Every Night
Lay the Favorite

FIREWORKS EVERY NIGHT

FIREWORKS EVERY NIGHT

A Novel

BETH RAYMER

RANDOM HOUSE

NEW YORK

Published in the United States by Random House,
an imprint and division of Penguin Random House LLC, New York.

RANDOM HOUSE and the HOUSE colophon are
registered trademarks of Penguin Random House LLC.

Library of Congress Cataloging-in-Publication Data
Names: Raymer, Beth, author.
Title: Fireworks every night: a novel / Beth Raymer.
Description: New York: Random House, 2023.
Identifiers: LCCN 2023001467 (print) | LCCN 2023001468 (ebook) |
ISBN 9780812993165 (hardcover) | ISBN 9780679644712 (ebook)
Subjects: LCSH: Dysfunctional families—Fiction. |
Self-actualization (Psychology) in women—Fiction. |
Florida—Fiction. | LCGFT: Bildungsromans.
Classification: LCC PS3618.A984 F57 2023 (print) |
LCC PS3618.A984 (ebook) | DDC 813/.6—dc23/eng/20230227
LC record available at https://lccn.loc.gov/2023001467
LC ebook record available at https://lccn.loc.gov/2023001468

Printed in Canada on acid-free paper

randomhousebooks.com

2 4 6 8 9 7 5 3 1

First Edition

Book design by Elizabeth A. D. Eno

To Junior, for reminding me

". . . but I've seen the fireworks, haven't I,
sir?—it can't be fireworks *every* night."
—Henry James, "Brooksmith"

What is the human soul
but a claw pointing back
toward the forest

—Don Domanski,
"An Old Amphibious God," *Wolf-Ladder*

FIREWORKS EVERY NIGHT

THE SUN'S GOLDEN GLITTER THREW itself against Marie Antoinette's harp. Gilded with hand-painted flowers and depictions of Minerva, it stood in the corner against a wall of windows that commanded sweeping views of the Long Island Sound. To me, the harp seemed lonely—a party guest who doesn't know anyone, in desperate need of a drink. Every time I visited Alex's parents' house, I headed straight for it and plucked a string. The tension was so taut that it resonated without seeming to vibrate. The sound was akin to a bell, ringing out delicate and clear up to the double-height ceilings. I could never quite believe that Alex grew up with Marie Antoinette's harp in his living room. "It wasn't her main harp," he said. "I think she just strummed it a few times."

Like many other pieces in the Wellmans' art collection, the harp traveled often to different museums and conservatories around the world. It appeared, disappeared, went on tour.

For our engagement party, it reappears.

The event producer arrives. His assistants carry clusters of white flowers, tablecloths, enormous shapely vases. Parties of this caliber make me nervous. Someone stands for a speech, and I brace myself for a manic episode. I sit on anything white and I'm certain I'm going to start my period. Needing a drink, I open the liquor cabinet—crème de cassis, Campari. The Wellmans are not drinkers.

Mr. Wellman approaches. Mild-mannered, soft-spoken, he is the embodiment of a wise patriarch. He dozes in the rose garden. He reads up on wars. Anyone in the family has a question about tax shelters—they go to him. They have to make an appointment and everything.

Mr. Wellman is impeccably polite. To the point where I have a hard time telling how he really feels about anything. I once went with him, just the two of us, to buy a painting. The artist lived in a building in Hartford—an hour-and-a-half drive from Darien. I had never witnessed an art deal; I was under the assumption it would be a joyful event. The artist wouldn't come out of her kitchen, so Mr. Wellman negotiated with her boyfriend in the TV room. He was nice—he offered us coffee—but the artist kept shouting rude remarks. "Sure you want it? Think it's gonna match your sofa?" I was confused: why was she insulting a buyer, especially one as kind and generous as Mr. Wellman? I asked him about it on the drive home. "Well," he said and left it at that.

"There you are! Hello, dear," he says. I close the liquor cabinet.

"I have good news." He gauges my reaction, though he hasn't told me a thing. "Your mother's coming."

My face goes tingly and my breath cycles fast, as though I might faint. He must notice something in my expression, because he starts saying things like *We want to meet her. We've grown to love you. I'm sure we'll grow to love her as well. It will mean a lot to her to be involved. That's all any parent wants.*

By the time I find Alex, in a separate wing, in his childhood bedroom, laying out his suit on his childhood bed, I've broken into hives. They start at my chest, climb up the side of my neck, and creep around to the corner of my lip.

"Are you allergic to the hydrangeas?" he says.

"Did you invite my mom?"

He sucks in his cheeks. It's his tell; he does it whenever he knows he's done something somebody won't like.

"She RSVP'd. We got the email this morning."

I'm floored. She has email? My feeling is that there's been some kind of mistake. Like, he got in touch with the wrong Mary Kay Borkoski.

"What's her email?" I say.

"Why?"

"What is it?"

"MissPalmBeach at AOL."

I haven't seen my mom since I was seventeen—about nine years ago. Last I heard, she lives in Ohio and her job involves manual labor. Yet there's no doubt in my mind: that's definitely her email.

"My parents were concerned that the guest list was too lopsided," Alex says. "Your side was basically blank."

"There's a reason for that!" I hear panic in my voice.

Alex softens his tone. "My parents set everything up. It's all taken care of. They want you to feel represented. They feel like you don't have anyone. That's all."

Everything he's saying is profoundly embarrassing. Not having family support makes me feel like a reject—which is exactly why I wanted to elope to Vegas. But Alex wouldn't have it. He said that marriage was a time to "build our community"—if we had problems, in the future, we could turn to those who, in bearing witness, had sanctified our vows, and they would support us. I had never understood that to be the purpose of a wedding.

"I'm not prepared to see my mother. Especially in front of a crowd of people I barely know."

"This time tomorrow, you'll feel differently," he says with cool certainty. "Trust me."

I sit on the bed and watch him get dressed. I wonder if he's looked for or perhaps maybe even found my father. But I can't bring myself to ask. The doorbell rings. Guests arrive.

Dress damp with sweat, rash throbbing along my jawline, I stand in the corner beside Marie Antoinette's harp. We look out to the living room, to the growing sea of navy blazers and classic strands of pearls. The candles are lit; tuxedoed waiters offer glasses of wine. I down one.

I watch Alex mingle. He is so good at making people feel welcome. His hair freshly cut, smiling, he is courteous, charming, especially with the elderly guests, and there are so many elderly guests—people his parents have known for decades, people with whom his grandfather attended boarding school. Shaking hands, everyone looks happy. I down another wine. My hands get that floaty feeling, and I begin to feel ashamed of my behavior. The Wellmans are right. She *is* my mom. She *does* deserve to be here. I don't know why I didn't invite her. I guess I saw it as doing her a favor—I didn't want to put her in the position of having to make up excuses as to why she couldn't come.

Alex spots me. His smile grows wider. I'm lucky. He's going to force me to grow as a person. He's all-knowing. He waves me over.

The entrance hall is crowded. No sooner do I stop talking to one couple than I bump into another. In the course of conversation, I take small steps and work my way toward Alex. I move aside; I let people pass. One more wine and I visualize the house from my mom's point of view—standing out because of the way it's lit and the number of people going up to it. I don't want her to feel intimidated or self-conscious. Maybe I should wait outside for her.

The air smells like wet leaves. Cars round the turn, and the driveway seems to swim.

I don't want to seem rude or unappreciative, so I return to the party. People I've never seen before say, "There she is!" I fill our conversations with questions so that there's no time or space for them to ask me any. At the slightest lull, I go back outside. Foot traffic in the entrance hall dies down, until I'm the only person opening and closing the front door.

Dinner is served. The large, airy garden room has been transformed into a dimly lit communal dining space. Glass candelabras rise from tables covered in cloths and plates, layers of dark green and electric lime. There are crumbling classical sculptures, and lemons—so many lemons—some loose, some tumbling from bowls, and some hanging from lush trees. Guests recall stories from Yale Law, and I feel their body heat, the vibration of their laughs, the crackle of the skin as I cut into my duck confit. But, mostly, I feel Mom's empty chair beside me, as palpable and distracting as a tumor.

"Tell me, dear," says Grandma Wellman. She asks me a question, but my attention is on my racing heart, and I don't catch a word of it. I'm not sure how to ask her politely to repeat herself, so I say, "Let me think." I pretend to concentrate on my thoughts and hope someone will save me.

"Mary Kay Borkoski?"

My stomach drops. One of the assistants has pulled back the chair. The name plaque is in his hand. "Will she be joining us, or . . . ?"

"Uhhhh . . ." I say.

"It's your mother's chair, dear," says Grandma Wellman in a way that implies I'm drunk, which I am.

"I know, but I don't think she's coming."

"Of course she is." She waves away the assistant.

"Wait," I say.

"Your sister?" Grandpa Wellman says.

"No. My mom," I say.

"But your sister . . . She *is* with us?"

Is he asking if she's in attendance, or if she's still alive? Either way, I say nothing, afraid that if I open my mouth I may puke. Alex turns to the assistant. "You can leave it. Thanks."

The waiters serve the Chair dessert. They pour it espresso. The food and drink just sit there, and I think up excuses on my mother's behalf. I feel embarrassed: it's rude of me that she would do this. I feel furious with myself for falling for it. I feel guilty for the awkwardness it's causing. But, mostly, I

feel shame. It travels through me like a sweaty, spitting animal. I know what it wants: to fly around the ceiling, graceless
and fast, pegging lemons off people's faces. The urge to give
in to it is overwhelming. It's in pain and in need. It can't fly on
its own.

I smooth my napkin in my lap. Alex stands for his speech.
"A friend asked me, 'Is C.C. your dream girl? Is she everything you've ever wanted?' And I said: 'No. She's not. My
imagination is not that good.' "

There are "ahhh"s, all eyes on me, and I feel it in my gut:
Wow, did I pull one over on him.

I don't say my goodbyes. I don't thank anyone for coming.
I whisper to Alex, "I'll be right back," then pass out in his
childhood bed. I dream I'm on a roller coaster somewhere in
the middle of the Atlantic Ocean. The roller coaster doesn't
go fast; it just creeps along. But it's extremely high, and the
seats are upside down. Every time my cart wobbles, my head
tilts and I glimpse an aerial view of the United States. But it's
Florida that really shines. Its outline sparkles like sand; I feel
myself gasp at its beauty. For what seems like the entire night,
I dangle in the sky, feeling crazily afraid, while forcing myself
to lean back, just a little, so I can see Florida.

The garden room is back to normal: one round table, four
chairs, bright, heavy shadows on the hardwood floor. Mrs.
Wellman serves French toast. Mr. Wellman and Alex set aside
their respective sections of *The New York Times*. I sip my coffee. No one mentions a word about my mom not showing up,
which I guess is the polite thing to do.

2

INSIDE THE REST STOP, FLIES blackened the cloth swathed around a plate of sliced oranges. The woman behind the counter told me they were samples. I could take as many as I wanted and didn't have to pay. I stuffed two slices into my pockets, one in my mouth, and bit down. This was my first impression of Florida: everything was sweet and free.

I joined my family on a bench overlooking a prairie of saw grass that stood well above our heads. Lorraine held Snickers tight. A malnourished tabby with one chewed ear, he was the only feral cat to survive the fire that had destroyed our home and used-car dealership. We were proud of ourselves for rescuing Snickers, but he didn't seem to appreciate our efforts. He had spent the last twenty hours pawing at the car door, longing for his dumpster burned black to ashes, crying for all his dead friends. I offered him an orange slice.

Dad studied the road map, looking for a place we could live. The condos in Orlando didn't appeal to him: not enough privacy. The coast was too expensive. He penciled a route toward Lake Okeechobee, the big body of water dominating the bottom of the state. An airboat bearing an American flag roared through the saw grass. It was my first time seeing one, and I felt both scared and thrilled by its military-like energy. Snickers flattened his ears. Mom fussed with the tight red bun resting atop her head like an apple waiting to be shot. "Where the hell are we?" she said, face lifted toward the sun, eyes closed.

Under the overpass, we merged onto a two-lane road pocked with puddles. On either side, short trees sprouted from black muck. Even with the T-tops on and A/C running, Lorraine and I got broiled by the sun. There wasn't much room for us in the hatch of our brandy-brown Corvette. Not the most practical vehicle for two parents and two girls, ages seven and nine, but Dad liked cars with curves. We came up behind a station wagon that looked like it was held together with mud. Milk crates filled with strawberries and string beans were lashed to the roof. From behind the busted-out windows, faces peered. "Migrant pickers," Dad said, and gassed it past them.

We assumed we'd see Lake Okeechobee from the car. But after driving for two hours, we realized we somehow must've missed it. Swampland gave way to sugarcane fields. Mom got mad at us for bickering about the radio. Dad turned it off. "Peace and quiet," he said.

Lorraine tossed her long brown ponytail, so silky and fine

that her scrunchie slipped right out. I knew what the toss meant. She knock-knocked on the cooler. I make-believe opened a door. "Hey. It's me," she said, heavy on the mock despair. "I got somethin' I wanna tell you." She brought a spark plug to her mouth like a microphone. "I think we're alone now. There doesn't seem to be anyone a-ro-ound."

These were the only lines she knew, and she sang them over and over, looking out the window to the thick, scraggly woods for dramatic effect. I came in with backup: "Alone now-owww." Snickers meowed his high-pitched meow. Then stopped and meowed again. "Snickers, you are worse than a woman," Dad said, and he swore, the next place we saw, he didn't give a damn if it was a prison camp, that's where we would live.

Which is how we ended up in Loxahatchee.

A line of green plastic mailboxes wilting in the heat signaled that somebody lived somewhere. Dad hung a left. Along a narrow canal blooming with furry green algae, sapling limbs clutched at the 'Vette. High in the scruffy palm trees topped with sunshine were homemade wooden signs with a stenciled 1-800 number and the word "LOTS." At the end of a driveway, a fat man with a pink head buzzed to the scalp jabbed a shovel into the ground. Dad rolled to a stop and leaned out the window. He spoke over the engine. "Just drove down from up north. Work in the car business. Got two kids." He tossed a thumb back in our direction.

"This a good place to raise a family?" Mom said.

The man stepped a bare foot onto a shovelhead wet with blood, white guts, and waxy silver skin. "Depends," he said. "Whaddaya thinka rattlers?"

The lot we picked cost thirty-five hundred dollars. It smelled of rotten eggs. No roads led to it, but the seller promised that very soon there would be. Dad paid in cash.

The day before the excavation, we tied orange ribbons around the trees we wanted to keep. Through thick vine, over the soft circle of pine needles where the wild boar bedded down, muck oozed into my green glitter-jellies.

"That one!" Dad said. Afraid of snakes, he stood on the property's edge and pointed at trees that caught his eye. In this case: a tall silver palm. "That'll go on the corner of the pool."

Mom stood waist-deep in a palmetto bush. "Insurance money's coverin' *all* this?" she said. She waited for an answer.

"That one," Dad said, nodding to the low-growth shrub with leathery leaves. "Privacy. For the hot tub."

Dad acquired a pop-up tent trailer and we moved into the Lion Country Safari KOA: the cheapest housing option around while our home was being built. Outside our tent screen stretched taut against mosquitoes, gators snarled like chain saws. Mom didn't believe the sounds were real. She thought they were recordings piped through speakers hidden in the bushes. I insisted we keep Snickers inside the tent at all times.

Opportunity. I had never heard the word before and suddenly Dad was pointing it out everywhere. In the developments rising out of the swamp, in the thickness of *The Palm Beach Post*'s classifieds. Seeing it for the first time, he let out a low whistle—just as he did when contestants on game shows won a shitload of money. Back in Adena, Ohio, job openings were found by scanning the obituaries.

Dad applied at dealerships during the day. Circling off I-95 into downtown West Palm was like hitting the car-lot jackpot, he said. They just kept coming. One after another. Open-air dealerships ablaze in showroom shine. Walter Smith Ford, Roger Dean Chevrolet, Braman Auto. And every last one of them had neglected the used-car end of their business.

The GMs gave it to Dad straight: There were cars to be sold. But finding intelligent, hardworking people who could be trusted with hundreds of thousands of dollars' worth of inventory was difficult. In West Palm, there was nothing but beach bums and drug addicts. They liked what they saw in Dad: a sharp-dressed Northerner with a strong work ethic and a young family. He took a job at Al Packer Ford, working on straight commission. They offered him a three-hundred-dollar sign-on bonus.

"Five hundred and I start today," he said.

Seven mornings a week, sunrise spilled like grapefruit juice across the sky. I patted dew from the 'Vette with a dish towel while Dad got ready for work. Sitting in the driver's seat in his Fruit of the Looms, he shook Tylenol from the bottle and swallowed them dry. Drops of Visine, quick swipes of deodorant, a gurgle of Listerine that he spit in the dirt. He turned his cheek left, right, admiring himself in the rearview mirror. He looked good. Needed some crown work, that was about it. From the hatch, he pulled a dry-cleaned suit wrapped in plastic. He stepped into black pants with a sharp crease, buttoned his long-sleeved crisp white polo, and knotted a colorful tie. His suit jacket—black with a nipped-in waist and rolled shoulder—yanked him into a soldierly posture. He pulled on his Size 13 crocodile-skin boots, which he'd bought on the side of the road from a real Indian. Gliding a Dustbuster over himself, he removed specks of sand. A wink good-bye, and Dad backed out of the campsite.

Mom, Lorraine, and I played Uno and Memory until the afternoon heat forced us out of the tent and into the pavilion. Lizards vanished into walls. Mom chatted with fellow campers: retired couples with arthritis, workers from the sugarcane fields, surfers with construction jobs, single moms with long feather earrings, and teenagers with names like Clint and Clayton who knew all kinds of things about the Confederacy. Weekend campers came and went, leaving behind mounds of trash, which the boar threw up after eating. But we liked the long-term campers, with their calls to join them at the firepit for s'mores and Riunite. Like us, the long-term folks used the campground to regain footing after pitfalls: evictions, cancer, civil war in Guatemala. When Mom told them we lost everything in a fire, gifts appeared. Hand-me-down Barbies, books in Spanish, a badminton set.

Living in a hot tent with a cat who refused to use the litter box and two sweaty kids sharing a pillow and covered in insect bites was tough on Mom. No phone, television, car, mail, hospital. What made up for it was, for the first time in her life, she was making friends. In Adena, everyone had relatives. Here, nobody did. Every family we met was just like us: on their own and from somewhere else. The notion of friendship—of allowing people besides her sisters to give us rides to the store or the Laundromat—thrilled Mom. In a stranger's front seat, she turned around. Wind tossed her hair, and I rested my hand on the door handle ever so lightly and just in case. To be in public with her often felt dangerous— like we'd get lost, or talked into joining a cult, and never return home again. But then Mom unfurled her enormous smile, and I felt it too, the warm breeze as we drove out of the woods and into the bright sunshine.

We visited neighboring RVs for tarot-card readings and burritos stuffed with soft-shell turtle pulled straight from the canal. Mom learned how to play Bunco and how to apply Nair properly to her bikini line. It was heaven just to wander around the KOA in the matching leopard-print bikinis Dad bought the three of us at the Lion Country Safari gift shop. Our trip of the day was to Kobosko's roadside fruit stand. Mom sucked on a thick sugarcane stalk, compliments of Mr. Kobosko. Flatbed trucks zoomed by, and construction workers honked and whistled.

Lorraine and I spent hours perfecting our dance routines and performing them at the pool. A pregnant high-school girl taught us how to swim. The only body of water I'd ever been in was a strip pit. I would grab onto Dad's back and he would move smoothly and slowly through the cold, terrifyingly deep water. "Breathe," the high-school girl said, hand around my waist, and I came up for air. The smell of marijuana. Hard rock blasting on 103.5, the She.

I lived in the pool. Ate dinner in the pool. Ding Dongs in the deep end for dessert. Floating on my back, I caught every sunset. Even the moon was warm. In the bathhouse, dead animals clogged the toilets, and we washed our dishes in the shower. Naked and goose-bumped under the only spout that worked, the three of us took turns combing VO5 hot oil through one another's hair, as matted and tangled as the nature surrounding us. Down the narrow path that led to our campsite, cushioned with flowers that bloomed only at night, Mom held our hands while Lorraine and I sang the song that Dad played repeatedly, Crystal Gayle's "I'll Get Over You." I lifted my foot and took a dramatic step over an imaginary dead body. That's what I thought "get over you" meant. Why else would Crystal make such a big deal out of it?

Each time we visited our property, we came upon something new. A bevy of peacocks flying, despite their massive trains. Inspectors field-checking feral pigs, testing them for AIDS. Western Palm Beach County had the highest rate of occurrence in the country. Here, it wasn't just gay men getting it, it was women and children living in poverty, and mosquitoes and swine were spreading it, everyone was certain.

Floor poured. Windows installed. And, finally, a two-thousand-square-foot stucco English Tudor. It looked like something you'd find in a storybook—complete with a gable roof. Dad used his chin to balance the stack of Miller Lites he'd polished off while driving and unlocked the front door. I let Snickers out of his carrier so he could be the first to run in. I followed. It smelled of sawdust, hot and dry. My "wow"s echoed off the twelve-foot ceilings.

I couldn't run from room to room fast enough. Sunshine shot from the skylights, leaving triangles of white light on the thick, bouncy carpet. Construction dust covered the countertops. Windows still had their stickers. I pushed open the sliding glass door and dipped my foot into the pool: a perfect square of turquoise, with a hot tub and a slide.

I was the youngest; I don't know how I got the better bedroom. I think I just took it. It had a view of the driveway and, across the street, a flat brown stripe of canal. Lorraine ran in to tell me something and I made her leave, come back, and knock. I had my own door. I couldn't believe I had my own door!

We bought lawn chairs, Tupperware, a card table. One television, two mattresses. We lived like that until Dad got bonuses and we bought furniture. A flat bench, barbell, and weights appeared on the lanai. The garage got filled with roller skates, tools, and, finally, a car for Mom: a brand-new Mustang, black with neon-green trim. It was a demo—used by dealerships to promote sales in the community. As long as Mom kept the window sticker on, she could put as many miles on it as she wanted. On that first night Dad pulled it into the driveway, Mom self-consciously cupped her small chest. "I don't think I got the boobs to be drivin' this thing."

Living in Loxahatchee was the best life my childhood self could conceive of. There were a lot of other kids. Wild ones, who raced BMX bikes and had moms named Debbie and dads with full-back tattoos of Dale Earnhardt. Lorraine was a homebody. She read *Sweet Valley High* and watched *Days of Our Lives* with Mom. She was good with babies, and even at nine years old booked babysitting jobs easily. But she was also gullible. I'd trade stickers with her so fast she never realized she got the shitty end of the deal.

I preferred to be outside with the boys. We built forts with two-by-fours and supplies stolen from construction sites. At night we went hunting for "alligator eyes"; they glittered like rubies in the beam of a flashlight. I made sure to stay in front. A vet back at the KOA told me once: Leaders stir the snakes awake. Followers get bit.

Great white egrets stood with us at the bus stop. They beat their wings and we could feel the air move. Walking catfish covered in mucus barged out of storm drains on their hind legs. Wanting them to experience a better life, the kind of life

I had, I caught them, dropped them into a float, and pushed them around the pool. During rainy season, the roads flooded easily. The only way we could get around was by canoes, kayaks, or pool floats. Paddling to Publix for ice cream, I saw hundreds of thousands of fire ants holding one another's legs to form a living raft. Watching it float by felt like a spiritual message: things we kill 'cause they're annoying have brains and hope. As soon as I got home, I threw away the Raid.

In awe of the life we suddenly had, Mom, Lorraine, and I sat in the family room and admired the stone fireplace. I loved the *swoosh-swoosh* of the running dishwasher and the sound of the sprinklers kicking on in the middle of the night. "Your father is a provider," Mom said a lot. "Your father is an *excellent* provider." To show our appreciation, we planted lime trees in the backyard so he could have fresh ones in his gin and tonics. We painted their trunks white to protect them from sunburn.

3.

DAD SOLD CARS SEVEN DAYS a week, from eight in the morning until nine at night. Under no circumstances, other than being fired (or quitting—which also happened a lot), would his car be in the driveway during daylight hours. Within minutes of walking through the door, he fell asleep on the couch in his work clothes, white antacid flakes crusting the corners of his mouth, Snickers curled into his side. On his one day off per month, the two of us drove to the Palm Beach Mall and I helped Dad build his clientele. Shoppers strolled out of Lord & Taylor, and we handed them flyers, complete with Dad's head shot. "A car man you can trust," I said, and stuffed them into hands. Dad didn't approach anyone with a flyer—women flocked to him. "I got a few Mustangs on the lot still under warranty. You'd look good in one. Come see me."

The real world is worth experiencing. That's what my fifth-grade teacher told the class, and that was the pitch I gave Dad. He was skeptical: "Bev Dodge is no place for kids, Pumpkin." But Mom didn't have a job, and if Dad didn't let me shadow him, I'd completely miss out on Take Your Daughter to Work Day. "Come on, Dad. *Pleeeeeease?*"

I slipped rolled-up bills into dozens of balloons and handed them to the secretaries. In their off-the-shoulder crop tops and big hoop earrings, they blew them up and hung them from the ceiling. The salesman who had sold the most cars the day before (Dad) stuck a pin into the balloon of his choice. Pop! Money dropped. "Anybody who sells a car before ten A.M. gets a three-hundred-dollar bonus!" the GM yelled, and Dad strutted out the door. I followed.

In the ninety-degree heat with 100-percent humidity, Dad immediately stepped into the role of teacher. "Look for sure things," he said, either a man by himself who didn't need a wife's approval (he'd buy on emotion after the test drive) or a person who looked like they had poor credit and needed a vehicle. Say, a pregnant woman in flip-flops struggling to get out of a beater. People like that didn't care about aesthetics, Dad said. They just needed something to fit their budget. We could help with that.

The first twenty seconds in a customer's presence are the most important. For this very reason, I lagged behind—I didn't want to mess anything up. Dad approached with ease. "Welcome to Bev. Thanks for considering us. My name's Calvis."

Objections flew: Just shopping! Just looking!

He stretched out his arm and pulled me in. "This is my daughter. C.C. She's here for a school assignment. Wants to learn how her father puts a roof over her head."

I smiled. The customers seemed surprised: "Oh."

"We can save you money. Follow me," Dad said to one customer.

We sat at Dad's desk. He asked questions: *What are some things you like about the car you're driving now? You know your credit score offhand?* He considered their answers. "Gimme a few minutes," he said, "I got just the car for you."

At this point, Dad was supposed to check in with his boss to involve him in the selection process. But Dad didn't like checking in with anybody. He signed out a dealer tag, gave it to me to hold, and grabbed the keys.

We arrived at the car Dad wanted, blocked by another car. We turned around, walked the lot to get the key to move it, and returned to the car. He moved it out of the way and got into the car he wanted. I hopped in the back and set the dealer plate in the window. Dad wiped sweat from his face with a white handkerchief he kept neatly folded in his pocket. He cranked the A/C and turned the radio to a station he sensed the customer would like.

We pulled into the shade of the showroom. I stood to one side. Dad opened the car doors and popped the trunk and hood. This was called the "seagull." A sales method usually reserved to showcase the flash of European sports cars, it could make even a Chevy Nova Twin Cam look sharp. He pulled the driver's seat back as far as it could go. He walked inside to retrieve the customer.

Kindling the romance, Dad encouraged the customer to

touch the car. Feel the weight of the hood. "Go 'head. Slam it." He knocked on the steel safety cage and had the customer do the same. "In case of a rollover," Dad said, "God forbid."

The customer slid into the driver's seat. Dad crouched down, eye-level. He showed them how to adjust the steering and A/C controls. If the roof liner was thick, he had them rub it. Quality insulation makes for a quieter ride.

The dealership buzzed with aggression. The PA system was loud; salesmen stood in packs, smoking, dipping, spitting. Golf carts flew by; upset customers yelled. In order to fit the entire inventory, cars were parked extremely close together. The last thing Dad needed was a nervous customer to sideswipe a brand-new, fully loaded Dodge Daytona while pulling out for a test drive. Dad took the wheel so the customer could relax. I hopped into the back.

We stopped at the nearby gas station so Dad could switch places with the customer. "Take your time. Adjust the mirrors," Dad said, and handed them the seatbelt.

If the car had pickup, Dad would direct the customer onto the interstate. If not, he'd have them turn onto A1A for a slow coast along the ocean. Here, the smooth road kept rattles to a minimum. Seagulls cruised beside us. Long, silky wings spread over the tin-colored sea. "Beautiful day out, ain't it?" Dad said. I wasn't sure if I should answer. I wanted to appear friendly, but I also felt shy. There was something very delicate-seeming about sales. Like, one wrong word or an out-of-place giggle and the dream Dad had created would collapse. To keep myself from talking, I bit the insides of my cheeks.

The best part about used cars is that they have personalities, pasts. They have stories, and stories sell. Some of Dad's stories were true and some were not. The previous owner was "older," never missed an oil change, and, for one reason or another, drove it only a few days a month. "Good guy. We've done business since," he said. He noted the vinyl bucket seats, the chrome rocker-panel molding. "You could hop from deal-ership to dealership and you'd never find another car any-where just like it." Taking mental ownership, the customer glanced at their reflection in the wing mirror. They turned up the radio: "I like this song."

Back at the lot, Dad would have customers park beside their trade-ins. Then he'd ask the closing question: "Other than the money, which one do you wanna drive home to-night?"

Answers ranged: *This one, but I don't know how much it is. Depends. How much can you give me for my trade?*

Dad said it slower: "Other than the money—"

They nodded.

"—which one do you wanna drive home tonight?"

This one, but . . .

Dad held his stare. "If we can agree on the terms, are you my newest client?"

"Okay."

"Is that a yes?"

"Yes."

"Let's take a look at your trade."

The enemy of the car deal: customers *always* think their trade-in is worth more than it is. For this reason, Dad had them stand right beside him as he did the evaluation. It was essential they be aware of just what a piece of shit he was dealing with.

Dad turned the ignition. Empty gas gauge: buying sign. He flipped on the A/C and held his palm an inch from the vent. Dad never knocked the trade. He let the customer do it. "How do I make it cold?" he said.

After that, no more words. Dad devalued by using touch. He flicked the rust, poked at every ding, and ran his fingertips real slow along the bald tires. Paying special attention to all things broken, Dad gave the horn a few more tries and jiggled windows that refused to roll down. He jotted down the mileage, underlined it hard. "Follow me," he said, and the customer did, looking hot and defeated.

To get the figures necessary to begin negotiations, Dad was supposed to visit his boss, but Dad whispered to me, "Screw the boss." We ducked into the break room so Dad could determine the trade-in value and set the price himself. Using the vending machine for support, he scribbled down the numbers. Around us, salesmen polished off wings left over from the midnight sale. They asked me: "You wanna sell cars one day?" I nodded. "You're learnin' from the master." One of them gave me a silver dollar. "Hang on to that and you'll never be arrested for vagrancy." Dad rolled coins into the vending machine. "Give 'em these. I'll be there in a second," he said.

I set the cold water and popcorn in front of the customer, and that's when I noticed it. Behind the Miami Dolphins Rolodex, and a framed picture of me and Lorraine reeling in a fish on Lake Okeechobee, was a framed newspaper clipping. "Borkoski Used Cars Destroyed in Three Alarm Fire," read the headline, and below it stood Dad in his winter coat, staring at rows of torched cars and a melted singlewide trailer.

He appeared, eyes wide and alert. "Good news! This is

what my manager came up with," he said. He turned the paper around for them to see.

More objections: *I need more for my trade. I need to think about it. I can't afford that.*

"What can you afford? You tell me," Dad said. He handed them the pencil.

I tried to pay attention, but my eyes kept drifting back to the clipping. Why did he have it there?

The rumor was that Dad burned down our dealership and home. I had a few memories of people (Uncle Jesse, mostly) bringing it up during get-togethers, always in an offhanded manner and when they were drunk. Usually, Dad defended himself. "I loved that dealership. I never would've burned it down." Or "It was the middle of winter; furnace was ancient." But if *Dad* was drunk, he'd say other things. "These small towns are where you wanna be from. Not where you wanna live," or, simply, "I was tired of shovelin' snow." As a family—me, Mom, Lorraine, and Dad—we never spoke of the fire. Not a word. Not how scary it was to wake up to cars exploding, or the destitution that followed. Everything was good in our house now. It was big, and we had a yard and Snickers. But this one thing about Dad and how he may have caused the destruction . . . I don't think any of us knew what to do with that information.

So what did he see in the clipping? Or what did he want others to see? That he was more than a car salesman? That he was once a car dealer? It was the only thing that came to mind, and up until this moment, I hadn't even grasped the difference. I had no idea Dad saw this job as a step down.

Or maybe he used the clipping for motivation. He'd owned

a business once and he would own one again. This was just the beginning.

Then something else formed in my head: *Maybe he's proud of burning it down.*

The customer seemed confused. Or worried. I couldn't tell. Dad leaned in. "I don't wanna be goin' back and forth with my manager all day. I'm the one who just spent two hours with you, me and my kid."

Expecting the customer to look at me, I smiled, but they stayed focused on Dad.

"I've got a pretty good idea of who you are and what you want," Dad said. "Write down how much you can spend, and I'll do whatever is necessary to make sure this deal happens."

He looked at the customer with sincerity. They bought it.

Not long after Take Your Daughter to Work Day, the telephone rang, which was unusual. Minutes later, Mom woke Lorraine and me up.

"Get dressed," she said.

"Where are we going?"

"Just get dressed."

"Why?"

"Must you two have a comeback for everything?" She started to scream a little.

We drove into a hazy sunrise. Mom pulled into the fairgrounds and off to a side street empty except for a few shopping carts. She threw the car into park and walked fast into a flat white building made of cinder block. "You got a fast car," I sang, but Lorraine didn't join in. Lorraine could not handle discord of any kind. The carpet in front of Mom and Dad's bedroom was worn and shredded from her pacing. She stared out the window and picked at her nails.

An hour later, out walked Mom, face pale and drawn. Dad was close behind, along with some of the salesmen from Bev Dodge. Their clothes were limp. One buddy was beaten up.

"Well?" I said, squeezing in to make room. "Are Florida jails nicer than the ones in Ohio?"

That got a laugh. "Jail's jail, Pumpkin." They smelled of alcohol.

Dad insisted on stopping at Mom's favorite breakfast spot: Benny's on the Beach.

Glass doors opened wide to the spray of the ocean. Waiters wore guayaberas. Dad ordered shit on a shingle. He gave Mom a nudge. His way of testing the waters, gauging her anger. "Whatcha eatin', honey?"

"I am not your honey. I am nothin' to you," Mom said.

The salesmen jumped in to help. They taught Lorraine and me a game, "Love To, But." The rules were simple: they were the customers, and Lorraine and I were the saleswomen who had to overcome the obstacles they threw at us.

"I'd love to buy this car from you, Ms. C.C. But you're not givin' me enough for my trade-in."

"You're right. It's never enough, Dale. I bet in the last fifty years no one has ever come into this dealership and said, 'You're giving me too much for my car,' but we'll get back to that."

Dale was impressed. "Very good, C.C."

"I'd love to buy this car right now, Ms. Lorraine, but I need my wife to come in and see it first."

Lorraine pressed her face into Mom. Dad gave it another shot. "Why don't you talk to me, hon?"

"You wanna talk so bad, Cal, why don't you tell your daughters about their father tryin' to pick up a whore last night."

"Stop. Hold hands," Lorraine said.

"Who told ya that bullshit? The guys at the station?" Dad said. He pretended to be confused, just like he did when he played dumb with the A/C that didn't work in the trade-in car.

"It was in the release form, stupid. It said right there how much you offered to pay for her."

"I can only put two hundred down!" said a salesman, quick and loud.

"Two hundred? Ya sure?" I said.

"Oh, I'm positive."

"She was a nice girl," Dad said.

"She's a whore. How nice can she be?" Mom said.

"What about that watch you're wearin'?" I said. "You wanna throw that in?"

"You can do that, Ms. C.C.?"

"Yeah. I guess. I don't know. I'm new. I'm gonna go ask my sales manager."

I opened and closed my invisible office door. I could feel Dad watching me. He worked a toothpick from one side of his mouth to the other. "Never tell the customer what you're gonna do," he said. "They'll tell you not to. Just do it."

4

MONEY'S NO OBJECT. THIS BECAME Dad's motto. He traded in the old 'Vette for a C4, thirty-fifth anniversary edition, candy-apple red, completely redesigned. Johnny Cash blasting, empty beer bottles clinking beneath his seat, he drove us on vacations to Key West, Key Largo, Marco Island, Captiva Island. *Money's no object* while boarding the glass-bottomed booze cruises, while ordering lobster dinners, and Key lime pie for dessert, while checking into resorts that had ocean views and their very own private beaches where we rented Jet Skis and snorkeled with manatees. *Money's no object* while handing over his credit card to pay for a big-screen TV, a Ping-Pong table. At Christmas, we set up a tall Douglas fir in the bay window, threw the tinsel strand by strand, and placed at the top a battery-powered angel in a golden robe who sang "Rejoice!" It was eighty degrees. Still, Dad lit the fireplace. Our living room got so hot that we put on bathing suits to open presents. Duraflame logs sparked, and Dad, in his trunks, took great joy in watching news reports of winter storms back home. During particularly bad snowfalls, he couldn't resist. He picked up the portable. "Don't rub it in their faces, Cal," Mom said, and he dialed his parents: "Hey! Ya snowed in?" He pretended to gulp for air. "Twenty-six inches!? Didn't know it was that bad." He reached for his eggnog and brandy. "Come visit. Florida, we got it all. Motor sports, ribs, beer. You can drive on the sand right on up to the ocean. Fireworks every night."

I could hear Grandma's voice coming through the receiver in a fragmented sort of way. Dad responded in monosyllables. He hung up. "Assholes."

Mom's family visited every chance they got. Exiting the Greyhound, her sisters arrived: Aunt Connie, Aunt Cookie, Aunt Sissy, and Aunt Vi, along with their husbands and a chosen few of their thirteen kids. Sleeping bags and air mattresses took up every corner of the house. Bathroom counters were covered with boxes of maxi pads and bottles of my uncles' blood-pressure medication. They couldn't pass me and Lorraine without hugging us and shrieking over the length of my hair ("It's touchin' your butt, C.C.!") or Lorraine's looks ("If it isn't Brooke Shields herself!"). Tall, with dark, bushy eyebrows and glass-green eyes, Lorraine got that all the time. Especially from men at the mall.

Like Mom, her sisters were excitable and got all fired up over things like dust ruffles. But that's where the similarities ended. Standing beside them, with their big gold crosses on heavy chains hanging down the front of their Steelers sweat-shirts, Mom looked glamorous. "Miss Palm Beach," they said, admiring her bouncy, layered Sassoon haircut, her snakeskin Coach purse with matching wallet.

In the kitchen, they oiled cake pans and jabbed Kools into ashtrays. Talking above the crackle of pork chops frying in their own fat, the sisters overflowed with gossip about so-and-so, who drowned in the strip pit, whose windows got bashed in with tire irons, whose baby got into the bleach.

"Yins ever watch *Cops*?" Mom said.

"Every night."

"Is Sonny's boy—"

"That was him."

"I thought so!"

Seeing my cousins was like a happy yet awkward reunion. They still spit and called each other "pussy," but now they had muscles and body odor. At nine, I was the youngest, but I still beat them at Ping-Pong. Short balls over the net, putting it away with a slam, their skills were sharp. But it didn't matter. My defense was impenetrable.

Lorraine positioned herself on the outskirts of the table, arm swung over the front of her Benetton sweatshirt. She didn't play Ping-Pong. Our cousins talked about dropping acid, stealing stereos, and Judas Priest's *Painkiller* Tour. Lorraine nodded along, as though she were familiar with those things. It was how she fit in.

Among the cousins who would come to visit us was a guy named Butch, who wasn't a cousin at all. He grew up across the street from Aunt Vi. He was raised by a drug-addicted single father and abandoned when he was seven years old. So

Aunt Vi took him in. Butch was now twenty-five and known as the Sponge, or simply Sponge. He had black curly hair, and biceps the size of cantaloupes. He was comfortable walking around in a Speedo. The Sponge didn't know how to read. In his company, I felt vigilant. Lorraine did, too. We anticipated his needs, even those that had nothing to do with letters, like laying down his beach towel nice and neat, and making him Pop-Tarts. Aside from Aunt Vi, who truly treated Butch like one of her own, no one else in the family showed him any special thoughtfulness, and Aunt Connie got mad at Lorraine and me for doing so. She referred to his illiteracy as a "conscious decision."

"It's easier for him to go through life spongin' off others than it is to learn how to read," she said, exhaling her Kool.

This piece of knowledge blew my mind. I couldn't tell if she was being wise or mean. After all, Butch had had a very difficult life.

"How do you know it's a conscious decision?" I said.

"If I told you I was twenty-five, never had a job, and still lived with a family that wasn't mine, who's been supporting me out of their grace and goodwill since I was a kid, would you think I was ignorant or lazy?"

I really didn't know. I couldn't wrap my head around it. She gave up waiting for my answer and stuffed her cigarette down the garbage disposal.

It was one thing for everyone to call the Sponge "the Sponge" behind his back, but when they called him that to his face I wanted to die. But he just grinned and made his chest muscles bounce, which made me think Aunt Connie was on to something.

In the pool, my uncles basket-tossed us. Using their bulky,

round shoulders for balance, we lowered ourselves into eight fat interlocked hands with a few missing fingers. I was the lightest, and they hurled me high into the air. At that weird moment of weightless pause, I saw all the roofs in Loxahatchee, covered in pine needles so dry they glimmered silver.

At night, we played cards. But Mom and my aunts could never settle down enough to concentrate on a game. Shuffling endlessly, they laughed, and gossiped, and talked about how much they missed their mommy and daddy—who they still called Mommy and Daddy. The more Bartles & Jaymes they drank, the louder they played Reba McEntire, and the more they made fun of Mom. That time the mourning dove smacked into the kitchen window, and she poured boiling water over it to put it out of its misery. How she thought that tadpoles turned into turtles, and that the Underground Railroad was an amusement park—like Cedar Point, but for Black people. But the biggest joke of all was how, when we lived in Adena, Mom didn't have a car.

"You were married to a car salesman!"

"I know it," Mom said.

"You lived on a car lot!"

"I didn't say I didn't," she said.

Mom was always a good sport at being the butt of jokes. She'd laugh along, Coke in hand, with an earnest "How'd everybody get so smart? Where the hell've I been?"

When Mom's sisters really wanted to provoke her, they'd recall stories from their childhood. How they waited for the road paver to spread fresh tar so they could unpeel it while it was still hot and chew it—the closest they ever came to bubble gum. How, for supper, they skinned groundhog. Extremely protective of her upbringing, and deeply ashamed of the poverty in which she grew up, Mom didn't like having us hear those stories. She'd bring it up later, out of her sisters' earshot. "I don't know what they're talkin' about, *groundhog*," she'd say, with a sweeping gesture of the hand. "I grew up with freezers full of sides of beef."

Lorraine once asked Mom why her sisters were so mean to her. I thought it was such a daring question. But Mom, in her bra and curlers, eyelids painted deadbolt-gold, didn't miss a beat: "That's what happens when ya have it all."

Once, Dad's family did visit. Preparations seemed critical. Instead of steaks from Publix, we bought thick, marbled ones from a butcher. He borrowed a brand-new Cadillac from the dealership. Dad offered me "sips," which he tended to do in times of peak stress. "Sip?" he said, and splashed whiskey into my Coke. "Sip?," handing me his gin and tonic over the waterline, hot-tub jets churning away. On the evening they were set to arrive, Dad skimmed the pool every five minutes, making sure it was clean of every last pine needle.

Grandpa Borkoski pulled up in his Buick Roadmaster, whitewall studded snow tires, dark, heavy coats blocking the windows. Out stepped Grandma, Aunt Wanda, Uncle Jacek, and our cousin Anna in her long lace-neck floral dress. Their hugs were short but tight. Aunt Wanda gave us a box of black walnuts that she had harvested herself. Dad gave a tour of the house. He turned on the pool light, which cycled from hot pink to neon green. The colors swept over their faces, and it felt indecent, like the Waltons had stumbled onto the set of *Miami Vice*. I helped Grandpa find an outlet for his nebulizer.

Dry powder sputtered into his face as his throat rattled and wheezed from black lung. An old-man version of Dad but devoid of flash, he wore brown polyester pants and shirt, with a brown plastic comb in the front pocket. I felt a natural love for him. But I also knew that he'd caused my dad a lot of pain. When people remembered my father as a boy, they remembered him black and blue. They also remembered him wearing dresses to school. Punishment for peeing the bed.

Dad took a few days off to spend time with them. An open-water limousine to Peanut Island, a day cruise to the Bahamas. Every outing we took was accompanied by champagne. "Last few years been a dream," Dad said, wind in hair. "Never imagined I'd be livin' the life I'm livin'." Grandpa looked out to the ocean. Aunt Wanda sipped very slowly, and Uncle Jacek made nervous jokes that I didn't understand about his janitor job's pension plan. Grandma, who stood on her feet all day long checking oil, washing windows, and gassing up people's cars, eyed the bill. She spit something, and I had this sinking feeling that Dad was going to get into trouble, or that he was already *in* trouble, or that we all were.

Dad insisted we have brunch in Palm Beach. As we crossed the drawbridge, cars grew progressively fancier, until every other one was a Bentley, a Jaguar, a Maserati. The nine of us were packed into the Cadillac, and I kept glancing at their faces. Were they impressed by anything? Were they having any fun at all? They stared ahead, not talking, with the windows on their side rolled up. We hit Ocean Avenue, our windows down to the sound of crashing waves, and Dad referred to the residents—Estée Lauder, Donald Trump, the Vanderbilts—as "our neighbors."

"Say hi to our neighbors, kids," Dad said.

They weren't exactly neighbors. We lived fifteen miles away. Still, I shouted into the wind, "Hiiiiiiiii!" A palace came into view, flags waving from its turrets. Doormen greeted us: "Welcome to the Breakers."

Sunlight danced on ice tubs filled with stone crab, snow crab, king crab. Chefs sliced rack of lamb and marbled rib roast. Tuxedoed waiters moved gracefully to the harp's weeping tune. Lorraine and I poured orange-blossom syrup over our white-chocolate pancakes. Dad took a big bite of his lobster thermidor. Mom tried lox for the first time. "This is delicious! Sure you don't want any?"

Grandma and Grandpa, Aunt Wanda and Uncle Jacek, even Anna, saw the prices and refused to order. In silence, they sipped their water.

Dad held up his Mimosa and signaled to the waiter: Keep 'em comin'.

After that, Dad's family refused to leave the house. No matter how warm the breeze or sparkling the pool, they gathered around the kitchen table, ate brown-sugar kielbasa and chocolate sheet cake, and listened to Christian radio. The Bible Quiz segment was interspersed with Amy Grant songs, which Anna knew by heart. At some point the station flipped, and for three hours straight they listened to *The Rush Limbaugh Show*. He seemed angry in the way WWF wrestlers seemed angry, and I couldn't understand why this wrestler had his own show or why Dad's family listened to it. Aunt Wanda couldn't believe that we had never heard of Rush Limbaugh. An expression of shock appeared on her face, then slowly turned to one of amusement. She laughed, and I didn't get it: what was so funny about that?

They took a bath. Anna went first. Then more hot water

was added to the same bathwater so Aunt Wanda could take her turn. Then Grandma. Then Uncle Jacek. And, finally, Grandpa bathed last, in the same water. Mom squirted Scrubbing Bubbles on the tub's dark ring. She saw me watching and shook her head as though I had asked a question. She shrugged. "Humble, backward people, kid."

Sunday morning, we woke up and they were already dressed for church. We hadn't been since setting foot on Florida soil, but we kept that to ourselves. From a sticky pew in the last row, it was obvious that nothing in Our Lady of the Pines—a cinderblock building twenty feet from a nudist colony—resembled St. Casimir's back in Adena. There were no cold white statues of the blessed mother, or crystalline cobalt stained-glass windows. It was a congregation of happy handshakes and beer bellies nestled inside Dolphins T-shirts, tucked in for the formal occasion. During what was usually a time reserved for silent prayer, when you could hear the sound of one hundred heads bowing, a group of musicians shake-rolled their tambourines. At the end of the alms collection, the bandleader used the talk box on his electric guitar to say, "Thank you," striking the last chord with such force that the dogs outside began to howl.

The car ride home was cramped and tense with tight muscles, jaws, and controlled breathing.

"That was not a Roman Catholic church," Grandma said.

Dad pulled his emergency whiskey from the glove box. Lorraine pressed her leg into mine and I pressed back. Our Morse code for: Oh shit, he took some swigs.

"Lemme ask ya," Dad said. "There *anything* you people like?"

They stared ahead, faces hanging. Lorraine pressed her leg harder.

"They're doin' some construction here," Mom said, looking out the window, trying to redirect the conversation.

"Whatever you like to do, tell me," Dad said.

Uncle Jacek averted his eyes.

"You wanna go bass fishin'? Dad? That somethin' you wanna do with your son?"

His voice spiraled up at the word "son," like he had cut himself. It was weird to hear him refer to himself as one.

Grandpa folded his white handkerchief, neat and slow.

"We didn't raise you like this," Grandma said.

"No shit," Dad said.

"Florida's corruptin' y'all," Aunt Wanda said. Then: "We pray for you."

I didn't get it. *They* were praying for *us*? Why? We'd made it out.

Dad let go of the steering wheel. He shook his hands in the air as if the Holy Spirit had appeared in front of the car and spooked him. We veered toward the narrow canal running alongside the road. Wading birds flew from the embankment. Lorraine squeezed my hand. "Cal," Mom said. Dad chuckled. He placed his hands back on the wheel.

5

I FOLLOWED ALEX DOWN THE curved staircase. "Happy to report, not a drop of water in the basement from any of the storms," the real-estate agent said. She opened the French doors that led to the kitchen, which looked like a den. Behind sleek wooden cabinetry, she pointed out the three refrigerators. One for wine, one for drinks other than wine, and one for produce. I didn't see a freezer. Alex had told me it was okay to ask questions during the viewing (just not to show emotion), but I didn't want to appear dumb by asking, "Where's the freezer?" I felt around, discreetly tapping cabinets, thinking maybe they would push open. I sensed the agent's eyes on me.

"Frozen food has fallen out of fashion," she said. "People eat fresh now, organically."

Embarrassed to be told the eating habits of my own species, I slithered into the dining room.

Mrs. Wellman told me not to focus on the home's price
(1.1 million dollars). She stressed the word "investment." "A
perfect starter home for the newlyweds," Mr. Wellman said,
and Alex agreed. Still, I couldn't bring myself to go along
with it. A home, to me, was something Alex and I would
work toward when we were ready. Not something that his
parents would give us as a wedding present. It was both in-
sanely generous of them and outright ludicrous—something
I'd have to express gratitude for every time I saw them for the
rest of my life. It seemed like a lot of pressure to be that indebted. But, more important: who would we be fooling? Alex
worked as a reporter for the *Hartford Courant*, which was
downsizing every month. I worked at the zoo. I was called the
"zoo storyteller," but really it was a sales position. Ardsley
was not a world-class zoo. No scarlet macaws or white Bengal tigers. We got "throwaways"—bears that had been hit by
cars, koalas with chlamydia. Every one of our turtles had her-
pes. That's where my job came in. To keep up attendance, I
gave a rosy spin. It was just like used-car sales: the story sold
the animal.

With CVs like ours and a combined monthly take-home
pay of fifty-five hundred dollars, how could we feel any pride
or joy living in a house that we obviously couldn't afford?
How could we feel like anything but total poseurs? How
could we—

"Okay! Geez," Alex said. "But, just so you know, it's very
common. A lot of people do it."

I found a rental on Craigslist. Twelve hundred a month for
the first floor of an old house in New Haven—a half-hour

drive to both our jobs and, in my opinion, the best place to live in Connecticut. Museums and dive bars, wings at Archie's, fit guys in Yale T-shirts, and that old industrial feel, New Haven was lively. I loved sitting on the steps outside the library, reading and drinking coffee, and attending a Monday-night workshop that I came across: Narrating Your Experience with the Non-Human World, which was taught by a published author. My classmates' emails ended in @yale.edu, @dartmouth.edu, @hotchkiss.edu, and it took me about twenty-eight seconds in their company to realize how far behind I was intellectually. Not in any kind of bad way. But the casual references to philosophers, the easy slips into other languages and lines from poems that simply popped into their heads, highlighted what Alex referred to as my "educational gaps." He was the one who taught me that the sun was a star, the Allies won World War II, and Joan of Arc was a real person (I thought she was fictional, like Princess Leia). Sometimes Alex was in awe of my ignorance: "Holy shit, how did you make it through college?"

"Easy," I explained. With a GPA of 2.0, I got my AA from community college, which, in Florida, guaranteed me admission into a state university—I just punched in my Social Security number and got accepted over the phone. I enrolled in a pilot program for disadvantaged kids called "the zero-textbook-cost degree." Not having to buy textbooks meant that I saved money, but it also meant that I didn't read. Or maybe I did and I don't remember. I was also working long hours in sales. Days after graduating from Florida State, I moved to Westport for a sales job. That's how I met the zoo director. He was a customer. It's the one great thing about being a saleswoman: if you possess goal-driven energy and listen in a manner that's alert and invested, lots of job offers come your way.

Alex couldn't believe that people with a 2.0 could get into college, but that's the rule in Florida, which I respect; it's democratic. He also didn't know what an AA was. Then there were other times I exposed my ignorance, and he went, un-fazed, "It's pronounced *Proost.*"

Anything intellectual, Alex knew best. He was perpetually correct. If he said it, it was so, I was certain. I knew this from the moment I met him, outside the Citgo. Hood up in the bright sun and bitterly cold air, he stared at his engine. Thick white milkshake oozed out of his head gasket. I was walking by when it caught my eye. I'd never seen anything like it.

"Oh my gosh," I said. "I think your engine is, like, pres-surizing your coolant."

"Emulsified oil," he said.

"That's what it's called?"

He looked at me and smiled. I liked his freckles. And his old Saab 900, too. I smiled back.

On our first few dates, all Alex did was teach me stuff. He knew so much about different countries, their histories, and philosophers. Had I ever read Wittgenstein? What about Sar-tre? "No," I said. "What did they say?" Out of excitement, and nerves (it was just a matter of time before I mispro-nounced something on the menu), I gulped down Beefeater martinis. Going pee, I noticed how aroused I was, the black lining of my underwear shiny with wetness.

With time, it became normal for me to make intellectual blunders and mispronounce words in front of Alex. I mean, there was no way to hide it; we were married. But I feared accidentally revealing my ignorance in front of anyone else. I transitioned our living room into "night school." Each season was a semester. Alex put together my syllabus. Our day-to-day was basically one long editing session that he took to naturally and that I desperately relied on. Anything I created with my brain—work presentations, press releases, stories for my writing class—I ran by Alex first. Only after he approved of my drafts would I let others see them. After I finished a book from his syllabus (he was really big on David McCullough), we would go out for drinks and discuss it. Then I'd have Alex tell me whether I sounded stupid.

Alex received a ten-thousand-dollar monthly disbursement from his family trust. Every year the annuity increased by 3 percent, and it would continue until he died. This money was distributed into a special account attached to his father's business (real estate, outlet malls), and overseen by an advisory. I found this out the first year we did our taxes together. I was stunned. "I told you I had this, babe," he said, and I guess he had—I had a faint memory of coming home drunk from a date and googling "tangible assets." But he hadn't shared actual numbers, and I didn't realize that it amounted to that much.

Even after I found out about the trust, we didn't talk about it. It had the energy of one of those mysterious autoimmune diseases in that it existed, it was confusing, and it stripped him of things that made life meaningful (spontaneity, for one—he was always having to consult first with his parents), but it wasn't the end of the world and things could definitely be worse. From what I gathered reading articles and user comments online, Alex's shame or indifference toward it was common. People who inherit a lot of money usually find it overwhelming. The money is always there to fall back on, to divert them, to cushion them. And because they don't have to succeed at something, they tend not to. Unless they have strong characters. Which Alex did. He was conscientious and hardworking. He simply did not fit the stereotype.

When the rent was due, I wrote the landlord a check for my half and Alex wrote a check for his. This just seemed like the natural, fair way to go about it, since his paycheck was just a little bit more than mine. I furnished our apartment with things I found on the street. In the big blue recycling bins, I found tapestries and rugs, a little silver Italian coffee-maker, and my prized item: a Free People winter coat with the four-hundred-dollar price tag still attached. The Westport Goodwill had so much overstock that there was a trash compactor attached to the store. It's where I found our porch swing and bamboo desk. As an undergrad, Alex had spent a year abroad in India. I think that's why he didn't mind sitting on a pouf while eating dinner on the built-in ironing board. Alex referred to our apartment as "authentic." At least at first.

I enjoyed making a home out of things that had been thrown away. But, more important, I took pride in the fact that our home, our lifestyle, reflected what *we* could afford, not what his family could afford for us. Believing that the secret to contentment was low overhead, I went to great lengths to ensure that, no matter what came my way, I could still support myself on a meager salary. Alex was wealthy, but I wasn't. We didn't have a joint bank account, because I didn't want one. I had credit-card debt (Alex didn't). I had student-loan debt (Alex didn't). Because I was the one with debt, I needed to know exactly how much money *I* (not we) had, so *I* could pay my bills. That was the only way I could follow my strict Suze Orman budget. Alex said my beliefs were holding us back from building a life together. Sometimes I thought he was right. It was as though my brain were in debtors' prison; I could feel the bars pressing against my frontal lobe. But what was I supposed to do? To depend on someone to cover my ordinary expenses seemed as dangerous as a payday loan.

Around the same time Alex lost his ATM card, I began to think of the trust as unmanly. Alex was a smart guy with a career of his own. Why did he still need his parents' money? He agreed. He did feel "out of step" with humanity. But traveling expanded his worldview, his Equinox membership was crucial to his well-being, and he wanted his (our) hypothetical kids to go to private school, like he had. He couldn't afford that stuff on a journalist's salary.

In Alex's circle of friends, this exact disjuncture was evident: their jobs did not correlate with their lifestyle. They didn't care. Neither did their spouses. No one cared but me. It struck me how good the couples were at fusing their lives. The wedding, the purchase of a home, renovations (always the renovations), the first baby. These events happened quickly—by age thirty-one—and seamlessly. No hang-ups of any kind. They were well matched, these couples, in that they were entirely at ease with perpetuating themselves. They felt worthy of others' charity, and it worked in their favor.

In Alex's family, it was old order across the board. The men drove. The women were chauffeured. They *never* talked about money. But, slowly, Mrs. Wellman started to—with me. I could tell when a financial-education talk was coming.

The casual invite. The pink macaroons on the table and the chairs pulled out, waiting for us. "Money gives you control of your life. It gives you choices," Mrs. Wellman said.

Every day, I saw women on the Merritt Parkway in their Range Rovers, windows up, diamonds on fingers, scarves around their necks. They didn't strike me as having *choices*. They seemed . . . beholden. But the single moms at Ardsley who used the discount codes so they and their kids could enjoy a free hot dog and the peacock exhibit at half-price— now, those were women who knew the feeling of the open road.

"Money gives you protection," Mrs. Wellman said. "You don't want too much exposure to the elements."

I thought that was such a weird way of putting it, but I envisioned exactly what she meant: skin cancer from waiting at the bus stop.

Every Bulk Garbage Day, I came across a few decent dressers. But I was holding out for *the one*. In the meantime, I hung our underwear from wooden pegs that I drilled into the bedroom wall. Alex never said anything about the pegs. He'd get out of the shower, grab his underwear, put them on, and that was that. But on the night we had his parents over for dinner, everything changed.

It was their first time in the apartment. Excited to show them the place, I gave them a tour. When they saw our underwear dangling from the pegs, they became visibly upset. Dinner was rushed. Conversation didn't flow. No one complimented my pork loin. Afterward, they took us directly to Design Within Reach.

The dresser that caught Alex's eye was long and sleek with a solid walnut frame. Of course, there was no tag, and since I was the only one interested in how much it cost, I had to suffer the indignity of asking the saleswoman, "What's the price on this one?"

It was fifty-three hundred dollars. Mrs. Wellman pulled me to the side. She rested her hand on my shoulder. "C.C. Please. Allow us this gesture."

I felt incredible pressure to say okay, to be grateful, and to stop needlessly stirring up trouble. But the dresser didn't go with our apartment. It didn't go with me. I felt like I was being gentrified. I also knew that this was exactly how the chipping away of independence begins. You buy one fifty-three-hundred-dollar dresser and before you know it it's spawned seventeen-hundred-dollar nightstands and a six-thousand-dollar headboard for a bed that you're not fucking in anymore.

Plus, the dresser weighed a ton. If I ever wanted to move it, I would have to depend on another person.

Alex appeared next to us. "I can't do it," I said. It sounded like an apology.

"It's being delivered on Tuesday," he said. The sternness in his voice surprised me.

Alex lost his ATM card while we were visiting his grandparents in New York City. We were on Central Park South when it happened. He kept checking his pockets. "Fuck. Fuck," he said with each touch. "Fuck!"

He used his phone to lock the card, but continued to look and act distraught. I had money on me. We were right near his grandparents' apartment. I didn't understand why it was such a big deal. But for Alex, being disconnected, even briefly, from his money made the color run from his face. And without meaning to, I had this thought: *Don't have a baby with him.*

At the zoo, we found our new, "must-see" coscoroba swan unresponsive in her pond. She was immediately put on supportive care and diagnosed with botulism. This was common among the water birds who came to us via FedEx. Wetlands are polluted by sewage, and elevated temperatures have created a vicious carcass-maggot cycle. Throw in an invasive snail (it takes only one) and it's bedlam. Botulism is the reason for the mass bird die-offs in the Great Lakes and the Sleeping Bear Dunes National Lakeshore. It's also why you never see pintail ducks anymore. In the next year, we'll probably lose a million or more birds to an outbreak. Still, "botulism" wasn't a word I was allowed to use at the zoo. It spreads panic.

Sitting beside the swan in the animal hospital, watching her struggle to breathe, I tried to come up with a story as to why she wouldn't be leading Sunday's children's parade when my phone rang. I didn't recognize the number, but it was a Florida area code. It was him. Somehow, I just knew it. I answered, "Hello?"

It had been ten years since I heard his voice. It sounded exactly the same. "Hey, kid, ya still alive?"

He stuck to small talk, and I went along with it. My father didn't like questions or people who asked them, and I didn't want to chase him away. He did share that the weather was beautiful. "Eighty-eight degrees, like I like it." Our conversation was short, no more than two minutes. Dad called the next day. And the day after that.

I didn't tell Alex about these phone calls—I think because

they didn't feel entirely real. It almost felt like my dad was calling me from another realm, and if I drew any attention to it, the calls would stop. It was like I was hiding a drug addiction. Or having an affair. At home, I kept my phone close. It rang, I saw the Florida number, and I hit "decline." I stepped outside and called the number back right away. During one conversation, I heard church bells. Our apartment was close enough to Yale that we heard the bells from Harkness Tower all the time. But church bells in Florida? Dad got off the phone quick. "Gotta run, Pumpkin!"

I googled him. A mug shot popped up. His offense was light: disorderly conduct. He smiled with his mouth shut. I'd never seen him do that.

He asked me to visit him. The lump in my throat wouldn't let me swallow. "Really? Okay," I said. He gave me the address, and I looked it up on Google Maps. It was a big empty field in Central Florida.

I immediately requested days off work. But I waited and waited to tell Alex. Finally, I couldn't wait any longer. Wearing my hiking backpack, I walked into the living room. He was watching *The Rachel Maddow Show*.

"Hey. I'm gonna go visit my father."

"Your father?"

"My dad."

He sat up. "You don't think this is something we should talk about?"

I clammed up, which made Alex more upset. He said he shared so much with me but there was no reciprocity. He was right. He was good at being open. I wasn't.

"I'm really hurt by this, C.C. Can you at least look at me?"

"When I get home, I'll be a better wife. I promise."

Alex didn't say goodbye. On my way to the door, I took off my wedding ring and hid it in the bookshelf. I didn't want my dad to see it and feel guilty for missing one of my life events.

I drove seventeen hours. I rolled the window down to warm, sticky air and the hefty smell of soil. I always missed Florida, and when I was there, I missed it the most.

The field was bigger and emptier than it had looked online. Farther down the road, I saw a low concrete building enclosed by a high chain-link fence. I pulled up the dirt driveway. There was a guard.

"I think my dad's here," I said. I wanted to ask what kind of place this was, but what kind of daughter doesn't know where her father lives?

He handed me a release form. "He ain't back by six, he loses his bunk." I signed at the "X."

Shopping carts collapsed into one another on burnt grass. A sign read IT IS HARD TO STUMBLE WHEN YOU ARE ON YOUR KNEES. I heard a whistle. "Pumpkin! Over here!" He was leaning against the fence. My heart almost stopped at the familiar tilt of his head.

I drove up beside him. His cheeks were puffy. His skin was chapped. He smiled with his mouth closed, just like in the mug shot. When he started to speak, I saw why. His mouth was a red cave defended by craggy white shards. What had happened to his crowns? He'd spent so much money on them; they'd looked so good.

"You're all in one piece, huh?" he said. I didn't know how to answer that.

"I guess so. Yeah!" I said.

"There's a few thieves living here," he said, as he tossed two black garbage bags into the back seat. They were scrawled with the number "114" in Wite-Out correction pen. He plopped into the passenger seat.

I drove in a loop as Dad gave a tour of the grounds. He called it "the Mission." He said it was a homeless shelter, a religious one. "It's like a timeshare. You just gotta play the game. I listen to their sales pitch about Jesus, then get back to my vacation."

That's where he slept, right there in the dorm. A lunch-special sign leaned against a tree: Taco Tuesday. "Three meals a day, they do my laundry, *and* there's no bitchin'," Dad said. "It's better than livin' with your mother!"

That made me feel a little better about all of this.

He pointed out the chapel, courtyard, pay phone, and, beside it, a bell tower that soared as high as the pine trees. Around it stood dozens of men. Hair caked to their heads, faces cut and bruised, jeans covered with plaster dust. They looked baffled, like they had just fallen through a trapdoor and were trying to figure out if they had a claim. They waved to us. I waved back. Dad didn't.

"We got Bible thumpers, drug addicts, immigrants," he said. "Everybody mixed together, you name it. Most these guys just got outta prison. Though you'd never know it by lookin' at 'em."

One guy sat on an overturned bucket, picking the dirt out of his toenails with a hotel key card.

"Beautiful day out! Ain't it, Pumpkin?"

A Miller Lite tallboy appeared in his hand. He cracked it

open. The sound of my childhood. I'm with my dad, I thought. I can't believe I'm with my dad!

"Turn right," he said. "I got us a few nights on the beach."

I passed the security shed, smiled at the guard, and put on my blinker. I drove for twenty minutes. We were really out in the middle of nowhere. I passed a sign warning people not to pick up hitchhikers.

"I get paid tomorrow," Dad was saying. "I got thirteen hundred dollars coming."

I was trying to listen to him, but something didn't feel right. What beach were we near? I started to think this might be a setup. I was ashamed for thinking such a thought. My palms got sweaty.

"We're gonna take a shortcut," he said. "It's called Pine Ridge. You wanna go left. Lotta nice places down this way."

I looked left. All I saw was a long dirt road and pine trees.

"Is there another shortcut we can take?" I said. I heard the nervousness in my voice. I wondered if Dad did.

"Nope," he said.

I sat there, idling.

"Are you sure we should go? The guy said you'd lose your bunk."

"I'll get it back."

My instincts screamed: Turn around! But I didn't want Dad to know I was afraid. I turned left.

The road stretched endlessly ahead of us. To control my nerves, I rolled my neck; I hummed. I took deep, uncomfortable breaths. Dad talked—since when had he become such a chatterbox?—but I didn't catch anything he was saying. The white noise in my head was loud.

We turned a curve. I spotted life: A six-foot blow-up shark hanging from a post. A T-Shirt Outlet. An ice-cream stand. And, just over the bridge, a beach so golden it glittered. "I splurged," Dad said, and I felt awful for thinking he would put me in danger. I thanked him.

It was a mint-green sixties seaside motel with a loud, outdoor happy hour. Dad insisted on bringing his garbage bags: "Don't wanna tempt the thieves." In the lobby, in line for check-in, I watched the lady at the counter look at the bags, me, Dad. She was unabashed in her staring, and I wondered if she was going to come up with a reason not to give us a room.

I remember coming upon homeless people when I was little. Sometimes they were harmless—beach bums with deep tans and cardboard signs. Other times they were scary— scratching, screaming at something invisible. My mom would get nervous and lock the car doors. But Dad would just shrug. "It happens."

Our room had two full beds and a balcony that overlooked the ocean. Dad immediately hopped into the shower. I wanted to look in his garbage bags, I wanted to see what he carried around. But to do so seemed almost blasphemous. Given his circumstances, I wanted to show him only respect.

Over the next three days, my father slept. Every few hours, he would wake up, apologize for sleeping, take a few sips of the water that I left on his nightstand, and fall back asleep. With each passing day, his face appeared more relaxed. His fists unclenched. Mouth open, he snored. It was a different snore than what I remembered. This one had a whistle to it. From his missing teeth, I guessed. Listening to it, I was overcome with a feeling of loss.

6

LOXAHATCHEE MIDDLE CONSISTED OF DOZENS OF wooden portables resting on cinder blocks in a soggy, freshly bulldozed field. There was no air conditioning. The canal stench made the air smell. Busy flies chewed our ankles. Alligators walked up the wheelchair ramp, and we'd shriek in excitement and fear. Our teacher stayed calm; she reminded us of a familiar statistic: as Floridians, we had a better chance of dying by legal execution than of a gator attack.

There was no cafeteria. We ate at our desks. There was no gym. But that didn't stop the social-studies teacher, Ms. K, from starting a girls' basketball team. Thirteen, then twelve, and finally ten of us met every day after school in the parking lot, beneath the hoop Ms. K bought with her own money and installed herself.

Ms. K wore chinos and chunky white high-tops on and off the court. She was young, short, brash, and often mistaken for a student. She took basketball seriously, and insisted we do, too. She taught us how to steal by ripping the ball from our hands, and how to box out by pushing her butt so hard into our stomachs it knocked the wind out of us. Setting picks, she drove her knee into our thighs. Playing defense, she clapped in our faces. She talked trash. One girl quit because of it. Parents complained. I worshipped her.

To the girls who didn't run onto the court at the beginning of practice, she snapped, "You're done," and sent them home. Running suicides beside us, she shouted to the slowest girl, "Why be last?" I Sharpied the quote on the bottom of my Converse. After practice—a hot, two-hour blur of pivots, bounce passes, and smothering defense drills to help us get used to pressure—I rode my bike to the park near my house and worked on my left-handed layups. I wouldn't allow myself to go home until I sank three free throws in a row. In my bedroom, I hung posters of my favorite athletes: Monica Seles, Steffi Graf, and Charles Barkley. It wasn't just that they excelled or were champions—they *dominated*. That's what I respected; that's what I wanted to do. Whenever my parents fought late into the night, I focused on Monica's, Steffi's, and Charles's determined faces. I dared myself to uncurl from my side, to pull my fingers from my ears, the covers off my skin. Eventually, my only protection from my mother's screaming outside my door was my breath and my thoughts. Giving myself over to fear became a little game for me. The more I was able to take control of my nervous system, the more confident I became.

It felt like I had unlocked a superpower. Suddenly, I had something I could unleash. Lorraine, on the other hand, wanted to hide under the bleachers with the scattered trash and wonder why she was born. "The guy over there didn't like when I blew my nose. He's giving me dirty looks." That's what it was like to be in public with her. At school, I would spot her with her teachers. She'd be right at their side, just like she was with Mom. And, just like Mom, they peeled her hands off their skirts and turned their backs to her, their eyes fully open, exasperated by the sheer amount of energy and patience she required.

She had a tough time making and keeping friends. Sleepovers happened once, and she was never invited back. Waiting for the phone to ring, she'd invent reasons why she didn't like so-and-so in the first place. They thought they were so great because they wore Guess jeans. They made fun of her behind her back. I hated her self-pity. I got on her about it. The sullenness, the big sad eyes, the constant crying that the whole world was against her. She was like a phony kid-version of a soap-opera actress. Other times, she looked so genuinely defeated I found it unbearable to witness. Right away, I felt guilty, thinking: *My poor sister. I need to be nicer.*

Lorraine's emotions controlled the house. Dad worked even longer hours to stay away from them, I tried to distract Lorraine from them, and Mom didn't know what to do with them. Some days, she left gifts on Lorraine's bed—an Esprit jean jacket, stirrup pants—or little notes inside Lorraine's lunchbox. Other days, Mom didn't have it in her to deal with Lorraine's onslaught of need. She locked herself in her room, and Lorraine would lose her shit and try to pop the lock. If that didn't work, she slammed the toilet seat down again and again. Eventually, she slammed it so hard that porcelain shards flew everywhere. Dad installed a new one. Mom went into the bathroom with him and closed the door. Lorraine and I stood in the hallway and eavesdropped.

"Please. Talk to your daughter."

"About what, Mary Kay? She's thirteen. It's normal."

"She is not normal, Cal. Believe me."

Lorraine turned to me, her teeth gleaming in the darkness.

"You wanna know what I was doin' when I was thirteen?" Dad said.

"You know, on Tuesday, I almost took my life," Mom said.

Tools clinked.

"I jumped out of the car on Southern Boulevard," Mom said.

"You didn't jump, Mom!" Lorraine said to the door. "You stepped out at the red light, and when it turned green you got back in."

The door flew open. Mom's hair was pulled back tight in a wide velvet band. Her face appeared exposed, livid.

"I. Jumped," she said.

I took off for my room. Lorraine stood her ground, insisting that Mom was only trying to get attention. Out of the myriad of differences between Lorraine and me, this was the biggest one: I dodged the draft. She went to war.

We raised enough money for uniforms. Orange and shiny, they said LOX in big white letters across our chests. Ms. K coached us in the art of the nonstop, high-energy, full-court press, and we played it against every school, every game. It made us look good by hiding our weaknesses. We were short. None of us had an outside shot. But putting pressure on our opponents, making sure they didn't catch the inbound pass in the first place: we could handle that. As often as not, the inbounding player panicked and threw the ball away. Or I intercepted the pass and went in for a layup. Or I intercepted the pass, they'd foul out of frustration, and I'd sink my free throws.

We spent a lot of time on the bus, traveling to play schools all over Palm Beach County. There was nothing quite like playing girls from Boca Raton. Their gyms had Olympic-sized pools and locker rooms lined with bottles of mouthwash and little wicker baskets full of tampons. With ponytails curled in big ringlets, the girls bounced up the court. Crouched in our defense position, we talked all kinds of shit. Ms. K disliked them as much as we did. Only against Boca teams did she let us run up the score.

Then there were schools like Pahokee and Belle Glade. Mold grew on the walls and ceilings. Broken toilets were used as garbage cans. Rats squealed in the dark, dank locker rooms as Ms. K gave us our pre-game pep talk. "We must come out strong. If we don't, we'll be annihilated." Pulling down rebounds, they swung elbows. When they lost possession, they punched us in the back. They pulled our hair and yanked us to the ground. But sometimes, because of their untreated asthma and increased fourth-quarter wheezing, we beat them. A collective moment of disbelief; we were then rushed into the locker room, and the school police escorted us off the premises. We piled into the bus and took off down State Road 880. Basketball season coincided with harvesting season, when growers burned their sugarcane fields. On both sides of the highway, orange flames shot from acres of standing stalks. Plumes of black smoke loomed overhead. People waited at bus stops with garbage bags over their heads to keep from inhaling the ash that fell from the sky and onto our windshield like a light, black snow.

That September was exceptionally hot. Lovebugs floated aimlessly while having sex in flight, and if you pulled them apart, they would die. After school, I waited for Lorraine in our usual spot by the bus loop. When she didn't show up, I ran outside the school gate to the Polar Cup truck that sold lemon ices. She wasn't there either. My only guess was that she'd gone home sick and Mom had forgotten to let me know. It felt weird to get on the bus without her. Lovebugs pelted the windows, leaving behind sticky smears.

The house felt empty. It smelled of Lemon Pledge. Snickers sat fascinated, following every move of the vacuum cleaner. Mom didn't look up, though I was sure she knew I was looking at her. She turned off the vacuum.

"Hi, Mom."

"Hey, kid." Her tone was crisp. She didn't look at me.

"Where's Lorraine?" I said.

She concentrated on wrapping the cord.

"Mom?"

I followed her into the kitchen. It was spotless. She wiped invisible crumbs from the counter and brushed her hands together over the trash.

"She moved back to Adena," she said.

"What are you talking about?" I said.

She threw up her hands. "She wanted to go, I let her go. Why? You think it was a bad idea?"

Lorraine's room felt like the room of a missing child. Everything remained just as it was on the day of her disappearance. Pink silk sheets messy on her waterbed, towels on the floor, a poster of Johnny Depp from *21 Jump Street*. Walking by, I'd get goose bumps.

If Dad got off work early, we went for a walk around the block. It was a new kind of family time. Mom walked with her arms crossed. Looking like her entire world had fallen apart, she talked about where Lorraine was living that week (my aunts took turns letting her stay on their couches) and the paperwork required so she could start ninth grade at Buckeye Local. Dad stared at the ground. "Place is a shithole. Give her two weeks. She'll be back," he said.

I really didn't get it. Why did Mom let Lorraine go? And if her being away upset Mom so much, why wasn't she demanding Lorraine come home? The expressions and the actions were not adding up. And why was Dad acting so casual? I felt anger on his behalf. A sense of betrayal. He'd risked prison to get us out of there, and his wife lets his daughter go back because she gets sad when her classmates talk shit about her Bongo jeans?

Two weeks became two months became four months. Each time the telephone rang, Mom ran to snatch it up. If it wasn't Lorraine, Mom cried. If it was Lorraine, Mom cried. Sometimes, Lorraine asked to talk to me. "Hey! You bein' on your best behavior?" she said, like she was suddenly thirty years old. I pictured her on a portable, beside a concrete, smoke-spewing, open-mouthed coal stack. I handed the phone back to Mom.

It felt like something was being kept from me, like a secret.

I started snooping. I wouldn't even wait for the garage door to bang shut. The second Mom grabbed her car keys and headed to Publix, I was off to their bedroom.

Rummaging through Mom's nightstand, I found the usual: thermometer, cough drops, prints of her high-school graduation picture. In Dad's: cinnamon Binaca, a shoehorn, old editions of Kelley Blue Books. Fruit of the Looms and Playtex bras were stuffed into dresser drawers. I pulled open the top one. Standing on my tiptoes, I felt the smooth steel frame of the shotgun. I took my time, tracing my finger along the trigger's loop until I scared myself enough to stop.

On the floor of the walk-in closet, behind the hamper, paper grocery bags stood upright, a dozen of them, rolled at the top. Inside were magazines called *Club*. Girls with feathered, side-swept bangs French-kissed each other. Vaginas spread between fingers gleamed like pink vinyl. On the last page, and in her own handwriting, the model-of-the-month filled in a questionnaire. Almost all the girls were from Ohio and now lived in Florida. Just like me.

Mom pulled me out of school early. Lorraine was at the airport.

"They sent her back," Mom said, fastening her seatbelt. I saw that her hands were shaking.

"What did she do?" I said.

"We'll find out."

I spotted Lorraine at the gate, standing in front of the windows. It was her posture that caught my eye. Shoulders hunched. One arm slung across her waist. The closer I got, the more different she looked. Her long, silky chestnut-brown hair was dyed black and cut into a spiky mullet. Her boobs, now huge, filled out a black T-shirt that read, in big red letters: KILL 'EM ALL.

I turned to Mom to see her reaction. She was still looking around, trying to find Lorraine.

"She's right there," I said.

"Where?"

"Right there."

I pointed.

"That's not her," Mom said. And then she gasped.

Lorraine's face was inflamed with purple cystic acne. She seemed embarrassed to see us. I hugged her, and she straightened slightly. "Hey, dude," she said. Her shirt reeked of cigarette smoke. Her body odor was strong, like cheese left in the sun.

I held my breath. What happened to Brooke Shields?

7.

LORRAINE DYED THE ROSE-COLORED CARPET in her bedroom black with food coloring. Headaches, period cramps, dizziness, every morning she came up with a reason not to go to school. So low on energy, she didn't even bother with deodorant. Rarely did she shower, and when she did it was just a ploy so she could smoke out the bathroom window. When she saw me having fun, or enjoying myself, she called me a goody-goody. When she saw me dribbling in the driveway, she called me a dyke. In stark sunlight, her high and pointy hair, so black it was blue, added another four inches to her extreme height. Thick black eye makeup crusted the corners of her eyes. She was no longer a mere annoyance. She was mean. When I was awarded trophies and ribbons, I smuggled them into my bedroom and shoved them under my bed. I couldn't risk her hating me any more than she already did.

A week shy of her eighth-grade graduation, she got suspended. On the afternoon it happened, I was getting my teeth cleaned. Mom and I came home to flashes on the answering machine. The school secretary, the vice-principal, the principal—they said it was important to call back before three. It was past five. A car door slammed. We ran to the window.

Lorraine was in the 'Vette, shaking her head, refusing to get out. Dad struggled to unlock her seatbelt. Finally, he succeeded. He frog-marched her through the front door.

"That's not what we were doing!" Lorraine cried when Dad said the word "sex." Lorraine made herself smaller. She looked at me in a way that said *Help*. I opened my palms to her: *How?*

Mom snatched Lorraine's spiked leather purse out of her hands and dumped it onto the table. "You're on drugs. You have to be," Mom said, rummaging through lipsticks, lighters, folded notes. She picked one, read it to herself, and handed it to Lorraine. "Read it out loud. I want your father to hear this," she said.

Holding the note, Lorraine pretended she couldn't make out her own handwriting. Then she pretended she couldn't pronounce some of the words. "Eat me out," she swore, was code for meeting at Burger King. "Blow job" meant something was wrong with a person's face—a deformity.

Desperate for things not to escalate, I nodded: *Yeah. That's what it means.*

Dad declared this "a woman's issue" and pushed the handling of it onto Mom. "You've lost it, kid. Now you're gonna lose it all," Mom said, ripping the shower curtain from the rings, the toilet paper from the roll. She removed Lorraine's door from its hinges and put it out for pickup. Lorraine's bedsheets, pillows, clothes, shoes, bras, our toothpaste—Mom stuffed it all into garbage bags and lined them along the hallway. If Lorraine wanted to retrieve one of her belongings from the garbage bag, she had to do a chore first. "Unload the dishwasher and you can change your underwear," Mom stipulated. Lorraine refused. Night after night, in the same Metallica T-shirt and purple silk underwear from Target, she sat on the bathroom counter and worked the zits on her chin with a sewing needle. I peed and dripped dry. I brushed my teeth with my finger. "Everybody thinks I'm a ho," she said.

Lorraine ended up having to repeat eighth grade, twice, and by this time I was in eighth grade, too. I came home from playing basketball and found Mom sitting at one end of the sectional couch and Lorraine at the other. *Geraldo* was muted. They stopped talking when they saw me. "What's going on?" I said.

"Nothin'. Just talkin'," Mom said.

I poured myself a glass of orange juice. I put my shoes and ball in the garage. When I came back into the living room, they were gone. I walked to my bedroom. The bathroom door was closed. I stood as close to it as I could without touching it.

"I'm not mad at you. Just tell me who did it," Mom said.

"No."

"I'm your mother, Lorraine. You need to tell me."

I tried to piece together what this was about. Did someone

steal something from Lorraine? Was she pregnant? My stomach reeled.

"Will you tell me if I guess?" Mom said.

"No," Lorraine said.

"Was it your father?"

"Mom! No!" Lorraine said.

Mom continued coming up with names. Mr. Swaab, our neighbor who drove the potato-chip truck. Mr. Edwards, our music teacher. Then:

"Butch?"

It had been a long time since I heard someone refer to the Sponge by his real name. It took me a second to realize who Mom was talking about.

"That's my guess, Lorraine. Butch."

Lorraine said something but I couldn't make out her words. She was crying too hard.

That night, after everyone went to bed, I wanted to talk to Lorraine. But my feeling was that she might want to be alone. I stood at the threshold of her room, where her black carpet met the hallway's beige, where there used to be a door. I pretended to knock.

"Hey, dude."

I joined her on the waterbed. To the slosh of tiny waves trapped inside plastic, we swayed. She was rolling a joint, which felt so new as to be otherworldly. I was surprised by how quickly she moved her fingers. Playing it cool, I pretended to read the lyrics from the CD case. "The Sponge forced me to have sex," she said.

I promised to never tell anyone, and she told me about the night in Ohio when the Sponge, who was twenty-seven, went into the living room, woke up Lorraine, who was thirteen, and asked her to come to his bedroom and listen to music. Lorraine followed him down the basement steps, her head a helmet of pink foam bedtime curlers that Aunt Vi had set her hair with earlier in the evening. Among the wall-mounted gun rack, the posters of Camaros, and the corn snake in the terrarium, the Sponge handed her a can of beer. She took a sip. He sidled up to her. He petted her leg. He climbed on top of her. His body was heavy and hot, and for a moment Lorraine thought he was playing around. She felt her underwear come down. His mouth on her vagina. It was her one chance to scream, and she didn't. She didn't want to wake up Aunt Vi.

The next morning, Lorraine picked at her breakfast. When the Sponge took a shower, Aunt Vi went down to the basement to make his bed. She came back upstairs holding the curlers and returned them to their case.

Lorraine removed a piece of pot leaf from her tongue. "Do you think Aunt Vi knows? She has to, right?" she said. I wasn't certain, but my guess was she did.

Do you think Aunt Vi told Uncle Rob? Do you think Aunt Vi told Aunt Connie? Or Aunt Sissy? Do you think Mom told Dad? This constant guessing game—who knew and who didn't—became a major source of anxiety and paranoia for Lorraine. The feeling that a lot of people knew she had been raped but no one was talking about it made her feel like even more of an outsider. It made her think that, secretly, she wasn't believed. Or that our relatives had sided with the Sponge. It was a scandal—it *was* a scandal—but it was silent and only played out in Lorraine's mind. When the phone rang and one of the aunts' numbers popped up on the caller ID, Lorraine and I would go into her room, stand side by side, and strain our ears to listen to Mom talk. "Oh, I didn't know that. . . . I've often thought that, too. . . . God works in mysterious ways. . . ." Lorraine would look at me with bugged-out eyes and whisper, "They're talking about the rape."

I nodded. *Yeah: they were talking about the rape.*

Maybe we were wrong, though. Maybe no one ever talked about the rape. Maybe Aunt Vi was totally clueless, and that's why she sent a Christmas card with a picture inside of the Sponge with his fiancée. But Mom *did* know. So what was she thinking when she hung the picture on the refrigerator? How was there any explaining *that*?

Lorraine stared at the picture. Her lip twitched.

I pulled it down and tore it in half, again and again, until it was bits of pieces of eyes and teeth and skin. In the kitchen trash, I mixed it with wet coffee grounds, and shut the lid.

Lorraine wanted a Camaro, and that's what Dad got her. Unlike Mom, he didn't take her angst, bad grades, and behavioral problems seriously. To him, she was a rebellious teenager, just as he had been. It was a trait that ran in the family. Black with black-tinted windows and black leather interior, the Camaro showed up on the lot, and Dad bought it below invoice. He surprised Lorraine with it in the driveway.

"Christ," Mom said, and Dad tossed Lorraine the keys. "Holy shit, dude," she said.

It was Lorraine's responsibility to get us to school. We rarely made it on time. She stopped to smoke pot with her friends in a damp little forest where the sun barely entered. Like Lorraine, her friends wore black concert T-shirts, smoked Winston Selects, and had been held back at some point, or many points. The ones that were too old to be in high school were kept in a portable far from "general population." That was the term they used. From the car, I watched them pass a joint. This was not my crowd. I played varsity basketball. I listened to the Cranberries. I wore denim jumpers from 5-7-9 and hot-pink Converse. For fun, I stood in the driveway and beat a tennis ball against the garage door.

High out of her mind, Lorraine would hop back into the Camaro and immediately pack a bowl. Exhaling from her Metallica tin homemade one-hitter, she sped up around corners and bounced us over speed bumps. Some kids got the munchies when they got high. Or had laughing fits, or deep thoughts. Lorraine wasn't like that. Her body gave off a low, steady vibration that made her eyeballs shake. It was like standing beside a refrigerator. Meeting eyes with her was risky; it could lead *anywhere*. A crying fit, a lashing out, a seemingly endless, sweaty panic attack—she made smoking pot look profoundly miserable, and she smoked it all day long.

Loxahatchee High was deep in the sticks. For the last stretch, we had to drive on rebar. In the shadow of a radio tower, porta-potties dotted a football field surrounded by barbed wire. Above all flew the flag: LOXAHATCHEE. LOVE IT AND LEAVE IT ALONE. Lorraine ripped into her parking space, pulled the brake, emptied her bowl, and stepped out. Following in her wake, I saw the power of her intimidation. Girls, and some boys, staggered or seemed to shrink when she passed. I could feel the reverberations of their shock or astonishment or fear or whatever it was. Whenever teachers discovered Lorraine was my sister, their eyes flew open.

Four thousand students jam-packed the halls. Armed police in wraparound shades rolled by in their golf carts. Their main job was to keep the rednecks from beating up the Black kids and the rednecks and the Black kids from beating up the white kids who were always trying to prove how Black they were. The skinheads were beyond controlling; no one could keep them from doing anything. If you threw a house party and they showed up, you called the cops on yourself, and tried to act normal until they showed up. If you were eating lunch in the cafeteria and they stormed in with their scowls, you simply set down your sandwich and waited to be slammed over the head with a chair. They ruled the school, and there was no getting rid of them. When the top ones got expelled or went to juvie, there were their younger brothers waiting in the shadows. Basically, the statistic my middle-school teacher had mentioned to us turned out to be true. By my sophomore year, one former classmate was on death row, one was on trial in front of a grand jury facing the electric chair, and none of us had been attacked by a gator. The only way to get and stay on any kind of track was to play sports or join chorus. Quit those and within a week you'd be stripping at T's Lounge. Lorraine went one way. I went another.

The feeling was that something out of control was happening, but nobody acknowledged it. There was shouting between Mom and Lorraine, and Mom and Dad about Lorraine, but it was never about her extreme mood swings, or how sometimes when she walked it didn't seem like she knew where she was going. The main concern was Lorraine's appearance. Mom refused to be seen with Lorraine in public if she was wearing a Metallica T-shirt. She wouldn't let Lorraine sit at the dinner table in a Metallica T-shirt.

"Eat in your room," Mom said. "Eat on the couch." Lorraine refused. She sat on the kitchen floor, cross-legged, mouth to plate. When Mom couldn't take it anymore, she piled the Metallica T-shirts on the grill, doused them with lighter fluid, and burned them. Lorraine got a job at McDonald's and bought more Metallica T-shirts.

Lorraine found a dealer, Bambi, who accepted trades: pot, acid, or pills for jeans. Bambi weighed three hundred pounds. She shopped in the size twenty-somethings. Lorraine couldn't steal to save her life. She pressured me to do it.

At the mall, inside Bambi's special store, I took one look at those Size 26 jeans and I knew there was no way I could shoplift clothing that big. Lorraine urged me to do a grab-n-go.

"You do it," I said.

"No, you. Haul ass, dude. You're the athletic one."

I looked around the store. It was well lit, not busy. If I got these jeans, there would be peace in the household. At least temporarily. "Meet me at Wet Seal in ten minutes," I said. "If I'm not there, go home."

Lorraine left the store looking guilty, and I pulled a pair of jeans from the stacked pile. Holding them in my armpit and pretending to browse, I moved from one stack of jeans to the next. I pulled out a few here and there and pretended to check out the stitching, the size of the pockets. I waited in the checkout line.

"Find everything okay?" the saleswoman said.

"Actually, I don't know if you can help me. My sister bought these last week." I pulled the jeans out from my armpit. "She didn't try them on first and they don't fit. She asked me to return them, but I don't have the receipt or bag or anything."

"I'm sorry, sweetie. Our refund policy doesn't allow that."

A short, fake moment of disappointment, then, "That's okay. I understand," and I walked out of the store, jeans in hand.

Lorraine had two speeds. She was either in a snoring, un-awakenable sleep or attacking someone. She got suspended for fighting so many times that, by the time she was seventeen, there was only one school in the county that would take her: Project Lazarus. An old white schoolhouse with three crosses made of PVC pipe rising from its dirt yard. I think someone at Project Lazarus must've mentioned something to Mom, because one morning, soon after Lorraine started there, she and I were getting ready in the bathroom, and Mom poked her head in. She said we didn't have to go to school. She said we were going to hit the mall instead. Lorraine turned the music up loud so we could talk.

"Capital Cunt has something up her sleeve," she said.

"Maybe she's trying to be nice," I said.

"Yeah, right. Watch this."

Lorraine headed for the door. I grabbed her wrist. "Don't. You're always in such a hurry to fight."

"Don't fuckin' insult me."

"It's not an insult. Relax. Let's just go. It could be fun."

Lorraine sat shotgun; I hopped into the back. We passed the bus stop with kids laughing and screaming. It felt weird to be going to the mall so early in the morning.

Lorraine played her Metallica CD, and for once Mom did not object. Without warning, with no blinker to speak of, Mom made a sharp left into Palms West Hospital. Lorraine, not as ignorant as I was about surprise drug tests, shouldered open the door. I saw the black pavement move fast underneath us. She's gonna jump, I thought. I could feel it.

Mom slammed on the brakes. Lorraine jumped. She landed hard in the grass and even rolled a little, just like in the movies. Mom pulled over and put on her hazards. We watched Lorraine get to her feet. In her tight, faded black Bongo jeans, zippered at the ankle, she was all legs. Ungainly, uncoordinated, cutting across State Road 441, dodging feed-delivery trucks and sixteen-wheelers, she raised her arm and shot Mom the bird.

"And she wants to know why *I'm* so rude?" Mom said.

Or maybe Lorraine was shooting me the bird. Maybe she thought I was somehow in cahoots with Mom. I stepped out of the car.

"Lemme guess. You're takin' your sister's side," Mom said. Disgusted with both of us, she drove off. I walked to the Burger King and stayed there all day, agonizing over how I'd be able to get Lorraine not to hate me or beat me up for something I hadn't done.

Lorraine started dating a guy named Victor. He had big Gothic letters tattooed on both sides of his neck: FTW. For the Win, I thought. No, Lorraine said: Fuck the World. Everyone at school knew Victor as the guy who could pull stop signs from the ground. Over Mom's dead body was Victor allowed to step foot in the house, so Lorraine moved out. On the afternoon it happened, she stuffed her belongings into garbage bags and carried them, one by one, out the front door. Her body vibrated. Her face twisted, jaw clenched, eyes darted. It gave me a sickening feeling to see her like that. I stood in the kitchen in a blind spot where she couldn't see me, but I could see her and Mom, who sat on the couch, pretending to watch *Oprah*. "You wanna go, go. Camaro's stayin' here," Mom said. She always stood up to Lorraine, even when Lorraine was high, and it made me so nervous for her. In my mind, it was best to leave Lorraine alone. Let her take the Camaro, then, in a week, find out where she was living and have it repossessed. But Mom didn't mind confrontation. Either that or she didn't realize Lorraine was high. Either way, I don't think it crossed her mind that Lorraine might kill her, which, to me, seemed like a real possibility. That's why I liked the blind spot. It gave me an unobstructed vantage point. If Lorraine decided at the last minute to pull a steak knife from the drawer and stab Mom, I could grab the portable, slip into the laundry room, into the garage, and out the side door. There'd be neighbors, emus, air, sky. I'd be able to call 911.

"You hear me?" Mom said.

Lorraine hauled the last garbage bag down the hallway.

"You take that car, there'll be—"

Lorraine slammed the door.

I ran to it, locked it, and ran to the window. Off Lorraine went into the world, cupping her hands around a lighter in the passenger side of a beat-up Trans Am, the word ROACH written across the windshield, leaving her beautiful Camaro behind.

I walked into the living room. The TV was off. Mom stared at the black screen, her eyes shining. I took Mom's hand. I thought: *I'm your daughter, too. I won't turn out like that.* But when I went to say it out loud, it felt like a jinx. Lorraine didn't just "turn out like that." Something happened to her.

In the still, abrupt quiet, I didn't say anything. I just held Mom's hand.

8.

I WAS SIXTEEN WHEN I fell in love at a keg party on 50th Street, which is where all the keg parties took place. It was so deep in the woods that cops didn't bother to drive out there. There were no landmarks, houses, stoplights. Just pitch-black for miles, then a street sign that reflected black: 50TH ST.

The parties were thrown by Bart Wiles, the strongest, most competent redneck at our school, and his dad, Mr. Wiles. They plopped kegs into industrial garbage cans and filled them with ice. They charged three dollars a cup and used the money to pay their mortgage. The decal on the back window of their truck read "Don't buy anything you can't eat and don't stick your hands anywhere you don't want to leave them." I liked that.

Mr. Wiles built little fires here and there so we could see. Someone blasted Cypress Hill from their car. Girls dropped Jolly Ranchers into their Zimas and sprayed their legs with OFF! Guys did bong hits and keg stands. A group of guys I'd never seen before approached the fire. One of them caught my eye. My age, I guessed. Messy blond hair pushed back from his face, long dark lashes, blue dazzle eyes.

"Where do you get the cups?" he said.

"Do you have three dollars? It's okay if you don't," I said.

I smiled, he smiled, and every cell in my body felt like it was going to explode. Like, if I accidentally brushed against something, I would combust entirely.

His friends headed to the keg, and he stayed with me at the fire. Light danced on his golden complexion. His face flickered in and out of view. Each time it reappeared, he looked even more handsome. For a long time, he didn't say anything. He didn't need to. His presence alone felt like conversation.

"What school do you go to?" I said. The words barely made it out of my mouth. My brain was broken.

"Gold Coast," he said.

It was the school for bad kids. Lorraine went there, but only for half a day. She got thrown out at lunch.

"I stole a car," he said.

More people gathered around the fire. Girls took double takes. They traded glances. Their glances looked a lot like a question: *Who's he?*

"A Jaguar," he said. "I drove it until I ran out of gas, and then my brothers picked me up. I didn't have a gun or anything."

I laughed. "Why would I think you had a gun?"

" 'Cause you're pretty," he said, a little embarrassed. "I'm Jay, by the way."

On our first date, we went to Singer Island. He laid down a bedsheet on the moonlit sand, and we French-kissed for five hours. I could feel everything: his strength, his heat, the shape of his body, hard chest, and harder dick. On our second date, he drew me a picture of a palm tree, with a palm tree beside it so that the palm tree wouldn't be lonely. On our third date, he introduced me to his mom. It was one o'clock in the morning and she was painting. In a strapless black dress, she straddled a bench. Her feet were placed far apart, like she was bracing herself, and she moved between two canvases. Just like Jay, she had a silky, physical ease. She was a single mom and dated a lot, and Jay worried about her. We would go out to eat or to a movie and he'd excuse himself to call his mom from a pay phone. If she didn't answer, he'd get a stomachache and we'd have to leave.

Jay's brothers were bad, just like Lorraine. Seventeen, eighteen, nineteen, and they already had babies and probation officers. His home life was just as embarrassing as mine, and I loved him for it.

Jay kept a logbook in his glove compartment. A record of all the work he'd done on his rusty ten-year-old Integra, using parts he found in the dump (fan belt, Honda Accord; air intake, Mitsubishi Eclipse), and lessons learned ("NEVER LET A BEARING SPIN WHEN DRYING IT"). Waiting in the passenger seat while he ran into 7-Eleven for a Yoo-hoo, I'd read it. On some pages, the blue-pen notes gave way to a black-ink personal diary. It read like an angry drill sergeant. "Focus! Get educated! You work full-time and don't have a

dime to your name. Grow up! You've been pathetic long
enough. There's more to life than trying to pretend you're
something you're not. You're dumb. You're gonna end up
like your father, drunk and alone watching boxing at three in
the morning."

To look at Jay, you would never guess he was filled with so
much turmoil. Besides the fact: none of it was true. He went
to school. He *was* getting educated. And on top of that, he
held down a full-time job. The reason he didn't have money
was that his mom needed help with bills. Also, when it came
to knowing things of importance, Jay knew a lot. Dealing
with car failure, often daily, had turned him into—I don't
know how else to put it—a master of life. He deep-dived into
fixing things. Motor on the ground, bare crankshaft in his
grip, Jay *cared* about what was broken. He listened to electri-
cal connections and searched for clues as to what made them
stop working in the first place. The way he stood ready to
repair and paused to consider a problem, the way he could
tell how many miles were left on a part just by looking at it—
that, to me, was the definition of masculine competence.

It was like Jay had no idea who he was.

On the logbook's very last page was "CAREER OPTIONS:
Golf ranger, DEA Agent, Mo—"

Jay pulled the logbook from my hand. "Why do you like
reading that?"

"Because. I like learning about you," I said.

I didn't dare tell my parents about Jay. I didn't want to
distract them from their problems—which seemed pretty
fucking big. But also: Lorraine was the boy-crazy one, not
me. I couldn't be. In my house, or at least in my mother's

psyche, boys meant V-necks, cigarettes, heavy metal, pot, STDs, the GED, hard drugs, and psych hospitals—in that order. Boys were dangerous and dirty, and turned you into a disrespectful liar. Every morning, Mom read *The Palm Beach Post,* coffee and scissors beside her, ready to cut out the headline with my name. "Borkoski Rallies Loxahatchee Past Santaluces," "Borkoski Powers Lady Oranges to District Championship." She placed the headlines in the scrapbook she'd created, which was a big, thick family photo album. That's what it said on the front: FAMILY PHOTO ALBUM. And that's what I represented: the family. I kept the peace, the secrets. I brought the laughter, ease, and pride, and I knew on a primitive level that everything would change the moment I brought a boy through the front door. Eyes would still be on me, but in a suspicious way. Sneaking around, lying, I felt like one of those teenage girls you hear about who hide their pregnancies for nine months. I now understood exactly where they were coming from. The urge to conceal isn't always about shame. Sometimes it's about self-preservation. I'd arrange to meet Jay at a certain time, sneak out my window, and run as fast as I could to his rusty red Integra, which would be idling, lights off, down the street.

Jay worked as a caddie at Binks Forest. On moonless nights we took out a golf cart. I stood on the back and held on to the golf bag straps. Jay whipped back and forth. Over grassy mounds, we dodged sprinklers and long, sleeping gators. On sudden turns, laughing, weight-shifting, we flew through the pines, and over the ninth green, where the most important moments of our relationship took place. It's where we first said I love you, where we fled when our parents fought, and where we first had sex. Boxed in by swamps and ponds, we kissed and I ground against the hot brass button of his Levi's. When it got too hot, we took off our shirts. Soaked in sweat, our bodies pressed into each other, it felt like we were underwater. He pulled my underwear to the side. I held on to the back of his damp neck. Sweat dripped down his hairline and over my fingers. His teeth pinned down his lower lip. He looked so greedy. Out of nowhere, he lifted me up just in time. Cum squiggled through the air. Fast, like those first boiling bubbles rising to the surface in a pot of hot water.

Flushed, happy, I stayed on top of him, my head on his chest, his heart pulsing against my ear.

"You know what I want right now?" I said.

"My dick again?"

"Orange juice."

The phone in my parents' room had a glitch. It was one of those see-through, light-up phones, and whenever a receiver was lifted in another room (the kitchen, my bedroom), it would flash neon-pink. Mom liked the glitch, because it alerted her to the fact that I had gotten on the phone. It was risky for me to make phone calls late at night. There was always the chance she'd be sleeping and wouldn't see the pink flash, but if she did see it, she'd pick up her phone and ask who I was speaking to. Therefore, I never called anybody late at night, especially Jay.

One night, the phone rang. It was very late, about two in the morning. *Lorraine's dead,* I thought, and answered it fast.

"Hello?"

"C.C., help me."

It was Lorraine. She was crying.

Mom picked up. "Hello?" she said.

The line was quiet. Mom hung up.

I waited a moment. "Lorraine?" I said. She wasn't there.

As I sat up in bed, my heart galloped, and I had a terrible feeling. I wanted to call Lorraine back, but if Mom saw the flash, she'd pick up the phone. I waited to see if maybe Lorraine would call again. She didn't. I got dressed.

I tiptoed down the dark hallway, stood outside Mom and Dad's bedroom door, and listened: silence. I went into the kitchen and checked the caller ID. Lorraine's number was the first to pop up. I erased it.

In the garage, Mom's Mustang was parked next to the Corvette. Both had the keys on the seat; both engines were loud. The garage door banged when it lifted *and* closed. The likelihood of one of these sounds' waking my parents was high. But if worse came to worst and they came out to the driveway demanding answers, I would tell them the truth: it was Lorraine who had called, and I was worried. The Mustang seemed like the better choice. Less flashy. The 'Vette caught people's eyes.

I manually opened the garage door. Afraid that its full weight would come crashing down, I placed the tall stepladder directly below it and slipped into the driver's seat. I held my breath, started the car, and backed down the driveway fast. It was my first time driving the Mustang. I was surprised by its pickup. I left it running in the street, removed the ladder, and closed the garage door.

I had my license, but I had never driven by myself at night. Each time headlights came toward me, I had this crazy feeling that I was going to lose control and crash into the oncoming car. Strip malls that seemed close by in daylight now felt very far away. It took all the courage in my body to make a left turn at the enormous intersection of Okeechobee and Palm Beach Lakes Boulevard.

Lorraine lived with Victor in a Section 8 duplex. I didn't like going there. But sometimes, if I didn't hear from her for a while, Dad would let me take the 'Vette to do a drive-by. Every so often, I took them to the mall and bought them supper at the food court. The last time I did, they were on pills and drooling and making no sense. I turned in to their driveway, and my headlights reflected back at me. Every window was covered in tinfoil.

I approached the front door, its corners dense with white spiderwebs. I tried the handle. It was unlocked. I opened the door a little.

"Lorraine? You okay?" I said.

"Hurtin'," she said. I gave the door a push. It opened to the living room.

It smelled like wet cat food. There was black stuff on the floor, and Lorraine was mopping. An air mattress was set up, and I saw Victor on top of it. He was wearing just his boxers, and there was black stuff all over him. His mouth was open. His eyes were open, too.

"Is he dead?" I said, and Lorraine started to cry. "Are you sure?" I said, and she cried harder. But it was hard to really know if he was dead. I kept thinking I saw the FTW tattoo on his neck pulse. I only really felt like Victor was dead when I started to feel scared of him. I was looking at him, but it felt like he was going to sneak up behind me.

I said we should call 911, but Lorraine didn't want to. She

was afraid the cops would come down on her. There was a warrant out for her arrest. She owed Cashland $1,050. They sued, and she missed her court date. She had a registered letter from the police in her room. She thought for sure they'd put her away. She begged me to help bury Victor. She was certain the two of us could do it ourselves.

I made Lorraine give me her drugs, her pills. I scattered them over the mattress. I stuffed shit into Victor's hands. I couldn't believe how blue his fingernails were, and I thought to myself: *I will never paint my nails with blue polish ever again.* She handed me a Tupperware. Inside were dozens of needles wearing tiny yellow caps. The hair stood up on my arms.

I pulled Lorraine into the bathroom. Tiny Ziploc bags and hollow ink pens floated in the toilet. She didn't have shampoo or soap, so I just made her sit down in the shower and rinsed her off.

"Nobody's gonna hook me up," she said.

"No."

"Pain doctor dropped me. OB-GYN dropped me."

"No."

"You won't help me?"

"No."

There were no towels. I used napkins from the kitchen to pat her dry. I helped her get dressed. Her whole body was shaking.

We carried out the garbage bags, the cleaning supplies, the Tupperware, the shitty mop. We threw them into the trunk, then into a dumpster behind a Publix. At a pay phone, I flicked tiny snails from the receiver and made Lorraine collect-call our relatives in Ohio. "Tell them Victor threw you out.

Tell them you're on the streets, no home to go back to, no place to move to," I said. Out of all the people she called, out of every person from both sides of our family, Grandpa Borkoski was the only one who said he'd take her in.

I called Victor's mom. On the first ring, she answered. I made my voice deep and said, "Your son OD'd. Call 911." And then I hung up.

I took Lorraine to the bus station. Together, we had money for a ticket. She was grinding her teeth, popping her knuckles, stretching her neck.

"Do you know what's gonna happen to me?" she said.

"What?"

"I don't know. That's why I'm asking you."

"I have no idea," I said.

No drugs, no cigarettes, no benzos, she walked toward the waiting room. She didn't carry her purse on her shoulder like a normal person. She dragged it behind her, like she was taking a dead cat for a walk.

I knew everything about Lorraine. The names of her doctors, what strip mall they were in, all the meds she was on, doses, too, her favorite Western Union location. I knew her bra size, concealer color, recurring dreams. I knew how much her rent was and where to send the check. What did she know about me? Or anyone? Nothing. She'd never even been to one of my basketball games. The opposite of addiction is not sobriety; it's connection with people. She'd lost all capability. Still, her lingering, sour smell in Mom's car was a crushing reminder that I had just released into the wild something sick and in need of care. What *was* going to happen to her?

The sunrise spread in every direction. I pulled in to the

driveway. The paper was in the grass, which meant Mom wasn't up yet. The lights were on in the kitchen, which meant Dad was. I slid open the laundry-room door. He stood at the coffeemaker in his work clothes. He looked at me, then at the clock on the microwave. He went back to making coffee.

"Something bad happened," I said.

He kept making coffee.

"Do you wanna know what it was?" I said.

"If you wanna tell me."

"Victor overdosed."

"He at the hospital?"

"No. He's dead on the floor of the apartment."

Dad measured the grounds. Flipped a switch.

"Lorraine's on a bus. She's going to Grandpa's."

"You call the cops?"

"No. I called his mom." Tears weren't falling, but speaking was becoming painful. "I disguised my voice and told her to call 911."

Dad looked at me. I thought for sure he was going to take me to the police station, to file a report or confess.

"Most people don't even do that, kid," he said. Then pretended he was late for work.

I went into the bathroom. I took off my clothes. But I felt too weak to take a shower. I lay flat on my back atop the cool white tile.

9.

I NO LONGER SLEPT THROUGH the night. I stopped straightening up the apartment. I didn't have the energy to hang up my jacket or open the mail. I tossed it on top of the refrigerator. I think I looked normal, but inside, I felt corroded. Like I was *allowing* my father to be homeless. I kept thinking of the men I saw at the homeless shelter who looked and behaved mentally ill. I couldn't understand how my father was okay living with people that sick. I called the guy who ran Dad's shelter, and social workers at the VA. I asked how I could take action to get Dad off the street. They were frank with me: "It isn't illegal to be homeless, just as it isn't illegal to return to an abusive lover. It's not what I would do; it's not what you would do. But it's what many people do."

"So what do I do?" I said.

"Pray."

I compulsively checked the weather in Florida. Anything over eighty degrees and I was certain my dad would have heatstroke. Hurricane season made me ill. Storms brewed in the Atlantic and I called Dad's pay phone in a panic. He spoke over the clamor of rain. "Don't worry 'bout me, Pumpkin. I was in the service. In a pup tent in the wilderness. This is no different."

The only time I felt okay about life was when I was actively learning about homelessness. I read every book recommended by the National Coalition for the Homeless, every homeless Reddit thread, subreddit thread, and *New York Times* article on homelessness, including every user comment. People's personal anecdotes related to the stories were great for helping me find more books and resources. There was a Croatian professor at Yale who gave public lectures through the Center for Faith & Culture. Speaking about modern homelessness, he said we were all displaced. Whether socially or existentially, most of us are without a home. Within five minutes, I fell in love with him.

I came to the conclusion that homelessness was the natural ending point in the circle of life. Even if you had a family, left for work at 7:30 A.M. every day of your life, competed furiously for—and won!—every bonus your workplace offered, chances were you would turn fifty-five, get hit hard by divorce, bad health, nostalgia, lose your grip on what was left of your job, and wind up on the streets. To think otherwise was the ultimate delusion. Whenever possible, I inserted homelessness into casual conversation. I loved to talk about the ease with which it happens.

Dad got thrown out of the homeless shelter. He wouldn't tell me why. The cops dropped him off at a jail diversion shelter. "I'm glad I got thrown out. All that Jesus, three times a day. New place is better," he said.

"It's called Bobby Jo's Triage Center," I said to Alex, over dinner. His eyes got big.

"That's not good!" he blurted out, mouth full.

"Why? What's not good about it?"

Realizing that I didn't know the definition of "triage," he took a moment to chew and swallow, contemplating whether to turn this moment into a learning opportunity.

"Alex, just tell me what it means. Don't make a big deal out of this."

He wiped his mouth, gained his composure. "Triage centers are used by doctors during war. It's a way to prioritize whose life is worth saving on the battlefield," he said.

"Okay. Thank you. I hadn't realized that."

Dad asked for money. At first, it was small amounts. Eighty dollars here, a hundred there. The nearest Western Union was inside a pawnshop. It was Alex's first time going to one. Belts of ammunition decorated the back wall. The agent started the process.

"Do you know the person who you're sending this to?"

"I do."

"And what's the reason for sending the money today?"

"My dad needs it." I flashed my Western Union promo code. Free ten dollars when you wire one hundred.

Waiting for confirmation, we browsed the cases. Sparkly trinkets slinked over one another like reptiles inside a terrarium. Gold Rolexes mounted chandelier earrings. Diamond rings lurked under military pocket watches. Balancing on a pile of bullion coins, a glass eye looked back at us. Its iris was gray, the pupil a tad dilated. The white part was painted with faint, squiggly red lines for a bloodshot look. The agent handed me the receipt. Walking back to the car, Alex put his arm around me.

At work meetings, I grew weary of spinning. Why couldn't we just be straight with the public? Animals didn't magically appear at our entrance gate. They were shipped here because they had lost their homes. Fires, droughts, development, invasive species—habitat loss was *the* primary threat to the survival of wildlife. Yes, our bears had been hit by cars, and they came to Ardsley to recover. *But* they were hit by cars because they came out of hibernation and there was no food resulting from the beetle outbreak stemming from the unusually warm winter. Hungry, they were crossing the interstate to break into a garage to get something to eat, and here came the Escalade (regarding collisions: wranglers included the make and model in the animal's file; it was always, without exception, a luxury SUV).

"I think we'd be doing the community a service if we just said, 'You know what, we're not a zoo. We're a homeless shelter for animals,'" I said from my spot at the round table.

"What do you do when you see a homeless person?" said the CFO. "You cross the street. We'll go broke."

"What about a homeless-shelter *exhibit*?" I said. "Each time an animal arrives, we focus on its homeless narrative, put it in the exhibit, and that's how we introduce the animal to the public. They meet the animal, they learn about its real-life circumstances; they see what it has gone through, why it has no home, no family."

"It highlights loneliness, which is something we want to

get away from," said Nick, my co-worker. "Visitors like to see animals playing in family groups."

"We've got the bats coming from Indiana," I said. "They'll be here by summer. We can give them human names and say they're siblings. They'd be perfect ambassadors for the homeless shelter."

"No money is going into marketing those bats. They're too charismatically challenged," said the CFO.

"Have you read the bios I put together? All the cave closures they've endured? Those bats are the mammal equivalent of out-of-work coal miners," I said.

My boss, who had been listening but had yet to say a word, crossed his legs. "It's very cynical, C.C."

My face blushed. I felt myself melt into my seat. I'd never been called that before. "How?" I said. It was a genuine question.

He lowered his head and looked at me over his glasses. It felt demeaning. I think he thought that I was being facetious, or that I knew better. But I wasn't. I didn't.

"Get our visitors excited about the star attractions, attendance will rise, and we'll be able to invest more in the threatened animals. Let's move on," he said.

My dad started asking for more money. The first time he asked for a thousand dollars, I think he detected my hesitance. It was 40 percent of my savings, but I did send him the money. "Increased demands" was something the homeless-parent subreddit posters often discussed.

"How much financial support do you give your homeless parent and how much money do you make?"

"Does our financial support help them?"

"AITA for not helping my homeless parent more?"

"What's AITA?" Alex said, resting his hands on my shoulders, staring with me into the blue glow of my laptop.

"Am I the asshole," I said.

Alex headed off to bed. "Don't get radicalized," he said.

My trips to Western Union became more frequent. I stopped bringing Alex with me; it was easier to just do it and not have to talk about it. One evening, when I came home, Alex was irate. He had found a Western Union receipt for six hundred dollars. Pounding garlic cloves with the hammer thing, he talked about how we needed to establish *ourselves*, plan *our* financial future. That it was my money I was giving my father didn't matter. It was the principle: I was throwing our resources into a black hole.

"I don't think of my father as a black hole," I said.

"I know you don't! That's the problem."

Maybe if Alex met my dad and talked to him, he would be jolted into understanding. About what, I wasn't exactly sure. Life? Grief? That my dad wasn't some sad sack? Why at least half of my mind was always thinking: *That's going to be me one day*?

"I think we should go to Florida. Together," I said.

Alex calmed down. "Okay, we can do that. We'll go," he said. Then: "I'd like that a lot, actually."

I am not a micromanager; at least, I don't think I am. But as we planned the trip, I felt myself becoming one. Suddenly, every little detail mattered. I was so afraid that Alex (and, by extension, I) would come off as snobby or insensitive or, at the very worst, obscene. I sat right beside Alex as he went online to reserve the room and rent the car. I just wanted to make absolutely sure he didn't book anything pretentious (no BMWs) or lame (no Mazdas). I made him click on the only car Dad would approve of: the Dodge Challenger.

I wondered if Alex had had similar anxious concerns when he first introduced me to his parents. Surely he did. I remember him gently steering me away from my jean skirts early in our relationship. That insight helped me feel better about the way I was acting. On the night before our flight to Orlando, I hid his loafers in the basement and begged him to leave behind his iPad. There was no way he would make a good impression on my father if he pulled that thing out. "I'm on deadline," he said, zipping it in its slim sleeve. "Let it be, will you, babe?"

It was Dad's idea to meet at the Dairy Queen. "For happy hour," he said, which I didn't understand. Alex and I arrived early, and Dad was already there, sitting in the back booth, beside his garbage bags. New ones—fresh, shiny, and black, thick heavy-duty, with handles. His way of making a good impression, I thought, and hugged him tight. He smelled like soap and was cleanly shaven, though his hair was the longest I'd ever seen it.

"This is Alex. I'm married to him," I said, still uncomfortable with the word "husband."

They shook hands. "Nice to meet ya, Alex."

The Dairy Queen happy hour was two-for-one anything you could suck through a straw. Dad said he could suck an ice cream through a straw. I said I could suck a hot dog through a straw, not realizing how dirty it sounded until the old guy beside us in cataract-surgery sunglasses perked up with a big smile. I shifted the attention to Alex. "What can you suck through a straw?" I said. "Uhhh . . ." He gave it some thought. "A root-beer float?" It was a good answer. "My treat," Dad said, and reached for his wallet. He handed Alex a ten-dollar bill, and Alex took the money. He headed to the counter to place our orders, and I could've fainted from relief. So much could've gone wrong in that conversation. Alex could've said he didn't want to suck anything through a straw, giving the impression he was too good for Dairy Queen. He could've refused Dad's money, denying Dad his dignity. But Alex handled it perfectly, and my confidence in him boosted.

The days that followed were some of the happiest in my life. It was stunning to me, a revelation, really, that I could have a relationship with my father even though he was homeless. I loved waking up with Alex, drinking coffee by the pool, and helping him transcribe his interviews. He'd file a story; we'd grab beach towels and head off to meet Dad. Bobby Jo's Triage was clean and orderly, one person to a room. It had the feeling of a minimum-security prison with a touch of homeyness. The doors were heavy, but there were lots of hard-boiled eggs in the refrigerator. In the lobby, there were packets of hot chocolate, a water cooler, and a big green marble table where the men played euchre and ate doughnuts. A bookshelf overflowed with my favorite genre: the criminal memoir. I noticed a copy of Assata Shakur's autobiography on Dad's nightstand. Never in my life had I seen him read a book.

"Wow! Dad!" I said, holding it up.

"Woman's got a hell of a story," he said.

Dad knew every beach, which meters were out of service

so we could park for free, and which 7-Eleven had the coldest beers. Alex bought us visors and beach chairs, which he set up for us so Dad could enjoy the booty-shake contest. Bad tattoos, loud New Yorkers talking about their pensions, and impossibly fast Shakira remixes blaring from a massive sound system was not the kind of beach day Alex enjoyed (he preferred quiet beaches, with lighthouses). Still, he seemed to enjoy himself, smiling at me every few minutes, nursing his Miller Lite.

For dinner, we went to crab shacks. "I'll just have a bowl of soup," Dad said, and I ordered him the all-you-can-eat snow crab. We drank strawberry daiquiris, with Myers's rum floaters, delicious! Key lime pie for dessert. Dad opened up a little, and I started to understand what his day-to-day life was like. His room at the Triage was free. He received a $189-a-month direct deposit from the VA, something to do with an explosion that happened in basic training thirty-six years ago. In the afternoons, he took a bus to a casino. It took him an hour and a half to get there, but he ate for free.

"Excellent food. They just give it to me," he said.

"Why do they just give you food?" Alex said.

My body tensed. Alex was well meaning, but he wasn't the most sensitive conversationalist. Sometimes it was as though he had learned his social skills by listening to *HARDTalk* on the BBC. At dinner parties, I often grabbed his knee beneath the table and reminded him in a whisper: "Conversation, not cross-examination."

"Well, I guess they don't just give it to me. I have to ask 'em for it," Dad said.

I ran into liquor stores in my bare feet, just like I used to, and they smelled just how I remembered: like stale cardboard. I bought Dad gin and lottery tickets. Alex actually read the lottery-ticket instructions—something I'd never seen anyone do—while Dad and I scratched away tiny gold bars, oysters, treasure chests. Get three of any symbol and we'd get three million, two million, one thousand a week for life! We passed dealerships and Dad became reflective.

"Always thought I was gonna end up a millionaire. . . . Ain't got the guts to do now what I did when I was thirty."

I reached into the back seat and held his hand.

"Oh well," he said. "Life goes on."

In the Triage parking lot, we said good night. We watched Dad walk by dozens of men with flannel shirts and tanned, worried faces. He motioned to the camera to be buzzed in. A cop opened the door. Dad turned around and waved.

"What made him think he was going to be a millionaire?" Alex said.

"Because he's an excellent salesman and a hard worker and a risk taker," I said. It felt weird to use the present tense, but I went with it.

Alex sighed, and I got upset. I thought we were having fun. I thought my father was doing well. "He's hanging in there," I said. "That's a lot."

Tension grew from Alex's questions. "Why do they just give you food?" had been innocent enough. But one afternoon, Dad was ripping through a twelve-pack and Alex asked him if he was "actively" looking for employment.

"Who you work for? Department of Labor?" Dad said.

To lighten the mood, I laughed.

"Have you considered going on antidepressants?" Alex said.

"N-n-n-nope," Dad said, and I shot Alex a look. Was he in a foreign country? Could he not read the street signs? The moment Alex headed to the ocean to cool off, I followed him.

"Why would you ask something like that?" I said. He was surprised that I was so upset. He said it was a normal question to ask someone who was struggling.

"You're meeting him for the first time, Alex. He's not a corrupt city official at a press conference who owes you anything."

"Well, somebody needs to bring it to his attention."

I walked back to Dad and sat down. "I'm sorry. He's . . ." I searched for the right word.

"Arrogant," Dad said. He cracked open another beer, shook his head. "Can't believe my kid married a Yankee."

From that moment forward, whenever Alex pulled out his iPad—to get directions, to look for restaurants—Dad chuckled. He began introducing Alex as his "secretary." To the waitresses at Denny's who seemed to know him well: "This is my daughter C.C. Alex, my secretary." And to the guys at the Triage: "You meet my secretary yet?"

"Your father is a stubborn old pigheaded son of a bitch who is as dumb as an ox," Alex said, getting into bed.

"I'd be nothing without him," I said.

"I can't tell if you're being ironic."

"The reason I'm here in a nice hotel, with all my teeth, having an articulate conversation, with you, is because of my father. Because of the shitty town he got us out of and because of everything he gave me. I feel grateful."

"Are you sure it's not guilt?"

"They're the same thing."

"They're not, actually."

"Yes. They are. What you're seeing is very normal, Alex. In America—not Darien, Connecticut, but America—people have dreams. They take chances. They make strides. Then they get hit by a car. They get cancer. They have a nervous breakdown. They don't age with the dignity they thought they would, and their kids step up."

"We all have blind spots, C.C. I understand that. I have them, too. But I feel like I'm talking to somebody who grew up in a cult. You need some serious deprogramming. Your father is not the victim here. He has made horrendous decisions."

"Who doesn't? So what? He made good decisions, too."

"He takes zero responsibility!"

"What do you want him to take responsibility for?"

"His drinking. Walking in and out of your life. What he did to your mother. His failures. His shortcomings. He owes you how much money?"

"I don't give him money thinking he's going to pay me back."

"Then why do you give it to him? So he can drink beer? So he can play the lottery?"

"So he can enjoy life a little bit! Yes!" My Lord.

"There's no reason he can't work. It's a con. He's conning you. Either that or he's having strokes. His whole sensibility is off."

"What makes you say that?" I said.

It was a genuine question. Alex just looked at me in exasperated disbelief.

On our last day in Florida, we stopped at the Triage. Alex shook Dad's hand, thanked him for the "unique experience," and walked out of his room. I lingered. Parting from Dad was difficult. I feared he would get stabbed. Or fall asleep in a park and teenagers would set him on fire for fun. It seemed to me only a matter of time until something that disastrous happened. Making sure to have "closure," I thanked him for the childhood he'd created for me. For his strength, resourcefulness, and all the risks he took and sacrifices he made to give me a better life.

"Noooooooo problem. Glad you came and saw me, Pumpkin."

Alex was waiting for me in the lobby. For some reason, he was sitting on the marble table. I walked past him, fast.

"*That's* what you're mad about!? That I sat on that *slab*?" he said, zigzagging through traffic to make it to the airport on time.

"It's their table!" I said.

"It weighed more than me!"

"Every table in your parents' house weighs more than me. You don't see me sitting on them," I said.

Alex laid on the horn, his face sunburned and peeling from the cheap sunblock I had insisted on buying at Family Dollar.

10

BY MY JUNIOR YEAR, DAD rarely made it home for dinner, and when he did, he was already drunk—walking in the door from work, juggling empty Miller Lite tallboys downed on the drive home, then tossing them into the trash and heading straight for the liquor cabinet. Just before opening it, he did a dance. Hunching his shoulders, he shook his hips, and flapped his elbows as though he were taking flight. If Mom and I indulged him, he stayed in a good mood. But if Mom was huffy to begin with, if she said "Cal" a little too sharply, or if we didn't laugh quickly enough, he stopped cold. "Okay. Noooo problem. Noooo fun allowed. Why have fun when you can bitch, right?" Overcome with guilt—he had tried to communicate his happiness and we blocked it—I would beg him to keep dancing. "Nope. Too late," he'd say. He pulled out the bottle of Jack. It made gulping sounds as it tumbled into Dad's drinking glass: an enormous ceramic beer stein airbrushed with Clydesdales galloping through snow. Dad threw in a few ice cubes and a splash of Coke. He polished off four steins a night.

Many times, Mom yelled—screamed, actually—"You're never here! When you are, you're drunk!"

"I work."

"You're a drunk."

"Somebody has to pay the bills. Ain't like you're gonna do it."

"You. Are. A. Drunk."

Dad chuckled. He cracked open a pistachio. And a beer, while he was at it.

He baited her, and Mom became so angry she lost her dignity. I remember her throwing dishes on the floor, hamburgers into the pool. And if Dad really wanted to send Mom over the edge, he'd call her a "taker." It was the cruelest insult, and I thought it was so unfair. Even with Lorraine long gone, and me having my own life, Dad still didn't want Mom to have a job—at least, that's what Mom said. Dad said that wasn't the case; Mom could work, she just didn't want to. I didn't know who was lying or who was telling the truth—I still don't know. But I do know that Mom spent each day cleaning an already spotless house, watching talk shows, and making dinner. In my eyes, she gave all she could, all she was capable of. Without her own income, she had no choice but to "take." How else would she eat? How else would she fill up her gas tank?

The mall was the only place for her to go, to get out—and stay out—of the house. Out of love, guilt, or maybe pity, I went with her.

"I'm trapped," she said.

"No, you're not. You can get a job."

"Your father doesn't want me workin'."

"Get a job during the day. He won't even know."

"Who's gonna hire a forty-year-old woman? What can I do? Babysit? Clean house?"

"Work at some place that sells dishes. Or makeup. You'd be good at that. Let's go to Bloomingdale's and pick up an application."

"I don't know how to work a cash register, C.C."

"They train you."

"Yeah, but you know me. I can't see crap without my glasses. Those little price tags."

"Then wear your glasses."

"If I work at the mall, I'm gonna have to take the turn-pike. Dollar toll, each way."

"I'll give you the two dollars, Mom."

She swept her bangs from her eyes. I wished for their divorce the way surfers wish for hurricanes.

Twice a week, at sunrise, I kissed Jay goodbye and sneaked up the driveway, bra stuffed into my back pocket. As softly as possible, I opened and closed the side garage door, the door to the laundry room, the door to the kitchen, headed straight to the bathroom, and took a shower as though I had just woken up and was getting a head start on my day. I had my covert operation down to a science. But then the doctor found a lump in Mom's breast.

It wasn't what we thought. Mom didn't have cancer. The biopsy came back benign. Days later, however, she returned from the mailbox holding an opened letter. Dad had taken out a million-dollar life-insurance policy on her. Mom took this as evidence that there was no love left. It was official: he wanted her dead. "What? Now that I don't have cancer, you're gonna kill me off?" Dad tried to reason with her. One day, no matter what, she was going to die. When that day came, a policy would help cover expenses and keep a roof over our heads. He didn't want to work forever. Calm, steady, he explained that he took the policy out behind her back because he knew she would never agree to it and it would just cause a fight. He said there was only one kind of person who would take offense at helping ease their family's burden: *a taker*.

The fight of all fights erupted. When it was over, Dad's cheek was covered in what looked to be road rash, and his nose pointed to the side. He plugged his nostril and blew. Black blood splattered the sink. Mom moved into my room. She brought her clothes, shoes, everything. Lorraine's old bedroom was sitting there, empty, but I didn't suggest Mom move in there. She seemed genuinely excited to be my "roommate" (that was the word she used), and I didn't want to do anything to burst that excitement or make her feel unwelcome—despite the fact that her moving in meant I could no longer sneak out with Jay. Mom mentioned many times how much she liked my room. It was bright, cheerful, inspiring. In my room, there were no bad memories.

It wasn't so much that I noticed a change in my mother—it was more like she expanded. Her long red hairs clogged my brush. Her perfumes covered my dresser and blocked my gold-fish from seeing out of its bowl. Her problems became front and center, her aggrievement profound. "Why did God give me your sister?" she asked out loud. "What did I ever see in your father?" She came to the conclusion that life had cheated her and she didn't know how, or even if, she could learn to live with the life she had. Desperate for answers, she turned to self-help books. Sitting up in bed, she read *Codependent No More*. "I wish this wasn't a library book. There's some things I'd like to underline," she said. Always a sound sleeper, Mom snored. Throughout the night, I felt her pressed against my side.

I listened to Mom. I remained positive, upbeat, encouraging. That was the easy part. What I found difficult was that, despite her all-consuming distress, she still tried to act parental. When I didn't make curfew, she grounded me. Claiming it was her right to know what I was up to, she went through my closet and drawers, which had become her closet and drawers, filled with her clothes and sandals. If she found something she disapproved of, she left it on the kitchen counter. I saw my new, sexy underwear that I'd shoplifted from Victoria's Secret the second I walked in the door.

"Got somethin' to tell me, kid?"

"You can have 'em," I said.

"I don't want 'em. I wanna know why *you* need 'em."

"They're underwear, Mom," I said, and threw them away.

She found my diary: a composition book that I kept in a shoebox. Rarely did I write in it. Mostly, I used it to analyze song lyrics, and occasionally to vent. One evening, I opened it up to my last entry. Atop my chicken scratch was my mother's sharp, medieval-looking Catholic-school cursive. It was like coming upon a pair of awkwardly positioned animals mating in the woods. It took my brain a moment to understand what I was looking at.

"Loxahatchee sucks," I had written. "It feels like I live in a terrarium, and no one is changing the mulch." It surprises me to recall writing this, because in my memory I feel I was always so mindful not to complain about anything, knowing how much worse it could be, and how good I had it. But I had complained, and Mom reacted. *I'll tell you what sucks,* she wrote. *It sucks that no one gave me anything close to what your father and I have given you and here you are bitching about it. It sucks that my life is half over and yours has just begun.*

Mom never brought up writing in my diary and I never confronted her. I didn't want to provoke a fight. I was noticing something about my mother: she was a victim, yes, but she also played the victim, even when she was the perpetrator. What do you do with someone like that?

I tossed the composition book into the shoebox and never wrote in it again, thinking: It's all yours, Mom.

Around the time of the diary, something else happened that I think I should've paid more attention to.

A sports bar named BJ's Corner opened in town. I knew the owner. I had coached his young daughters during a pee-wee basketball clinic, and he offered me a part-time job waiting tables. He hired some other girls in my grade as well. BJ's was packed every night. We never ID'd anybody. Jay would stop by to see me. After my shift, we drank Jack and Cokes, played pool, and had sex in his car. I'd clock out, and he'd drop me off at the end of my street.

On Friday and Saturday nights, I got home very late. Mom would still be awake, curled up on her side of the bed. I'd pull my wad of tips from my waitress pouch and set it inside my jewelry box. Sometimes the wad was so big that the jewelry box wouldn't shut. "Musta been busy," she'd say. Tired, and reeking of cigarettes, sex, and the soup of the day, I took a shower and soaked my tiny blue shorts, white tank top, and suntan-colored panty hose in Woolite. When I returned to my bedroom, the lights would be off—no "good night."

A few months into my job, Mom said I needed to quit. She didn't like me being around drunks and coming home at two in the morning. I loved my job, but I didn't put up a fight. I figured I'd keep the peace and, I hoped, return to BJ's come summer. Basketball season was around the corner, anyway.

When I went to pick up my last paycheck, I came upon Mom's car in the parking lot. My initial thought was that she was checking in with the owner, making sure that I'd really quit, or explaining why I had to. Feeling a little embarrassed, I went home.

That night, Mom and I watched TV. I didn't mention that I'd seen her car; she didn't say anything about stopping at BJ's. Dad came home from work. By the power in his walk, I could tell he was in a bad mood. Striding by us, he said, sternly, "Not a good look, Mary Kay. I don't need my wife workin' at a bar."

Confused, I looked to Mom for her reaction. She put her thumb on her nose and wiggled her fingers at Dad as he closed the bedroom door.

The gesture, so childish and old-fashioned—like something little kids did in black-and-white movies—grossed me out. Why was she doing that? "I can work wherever I damn well please," Mom said, and it dawned on me.

Just like the diary, I kept the revelation to myself that my mom had taken my job. It was too creepy to bring to light. Why did she do that behind my back, especially considering how supportive I had been of her getting a job? And of all places, why did she get a job at BJ's? It was a place for young people; she was by far the oldest employee, and definitely the only mom. My guess was that she was trying to show how pretty and youthful she still was—a message to herself that she still had it. Jay thought she saw it as a way of trapping my dad. "If he let you work there, she probably figured he'd have no say-so if she worked there."

My mom ended up working one hostess shift—a single lunch rush, from eleven to two—before Dad insisted that she quit. At school, my old co-workers approached me. They wanted to know what was going on. Why did I quit? Why did my mom work there? Why did she quit? I shook my head.

"It's too bad. I liked her," the busboy said. "She's hot."

I remember the queasiness I felt at his smile, and the Faith No More shirt he was wearing. The one with the great egret on the front, and on the back, a cow hanging on a meat hook.

With no job, I couldn't see Jay after my shift. With no privacy, I couldn't talk to Jay on the phone. And I certainly couldn't sneak out my window. "Just tell 'em," Jay said, growing impatient. "We're not doing anything wrong. What's the worst that can happen?"

I didn't know how to answer that question. It wasn't that I feared a particular disaster. I just couldn't imagine anything good coming of it. But maybe Jay was right. We were in love. No matter what, I had him. What *was* the worst that could happen?

○———— **11.** ————○

 I TOWEL-DRIED MY HAIR IN front of my mirror. Mom sat up, reading *Simple Abundance: 365 Days to a Balanced and Joyful Life*. She was on day three.

"This one's gonna be a problem for me, I can tell," she said.

"Why is that?"

"Well, they're callin' it *Simple Abundance,* but there's nothin' simple about it. Beauty, joy, order, harmony. How the hell am I gonna remember all that shit?" She used the little built-in ribbon bookmark to hold her place. I got into bed.

"Your father keeps telling me I'm crazy, but I like the person I am right now. I like livin' in here with you, readin' my books, not havin' to have sex."

"Mom."

"I know. You don't wanna hear it. He's your father. I understand."

Say it. Now. Now, I thought. I took in a long breath.

"Look at my next book." She showed me a copy of *Feel the Fear . . . and Do It Anyway.* "This one's gonna be good. This one's gonna be real good," she said.

"I have a boyfriend."

Mom turned on her side. She propped herself up by her elbow.

"Who?"

"Jay."

"Jay who?"

"Why is it important?"

"C.C., I am not letting you run around with some boy whose name I don't know."

"Newton."

"Jay Newton?" She thought about it. "Never heard of him."

"Why would you?"

"You'd be surprised how much I know. How long yins been an item?"

God, please make it stop. "Mom, I don't know."

"Why all this secretivity? If I had a boyfriend, I'd be happy. I'd be ecstatic."

"I am."

"He mistreatin' you?"

"No!"

"Then why are you holding everything in?"

She waited for an answer. I didn't have one.

"You know what I think?" she said.

"What?"

"I think your father and I need to meet this Jay Newton."

Jay's Integra pulled into the driveway, waxed for the occasion. I ran to the door before he could ring the bell.

"Hi."

"Hi."

He handed me a purple-dyed daisy that they sold at the 7-Eleven, and I tossed it into the bushes. No matter how ecstatic Mom told me I should be about having a boyfriend, I still felt it was best to play down our excitement for each other. Jay looked at me, confused. I said *Trust me* with my eyes.

I brought Jay over to Dad, who was lying on the couch.

"Dad, this is Jay."

"Hey, Jay. Nice to meet ya," he said, and went back to watching the game. "He fumbles the ball. Here comes Miami and . . . they . . . got it!"

I brought Jay into the kitchen. Mom had on her lobster-claw oven mitts. Stirring in the white wine, she was making cod puttanesca, her go-to dish.

"Mom, this is Jay."

"Hope you like fish, Jay. It ain't cheap," she said.

At the dinner table, Jay sat in Lorraine's old spot. Mom said grace. "Ayyyyyyy-men," Dad said, his mouth already full of food.

Jay couldn't have been more charming. In that bright, polite way of his, big smile, eyes sparkling, he complimented Mom's cooking, the house, the pool. He mentioned his job at the golf course and told Dad he could get him a few rounds for free—which Dad seemed genuinely interested in. He spoke briefly about the summer when he went to State Trooper Camp. Each time there was a lull in conversation, I said, "What else?"

Mom asked Jay about his family. Leaving out stints in prisons, state hospitals, the shooting up between the toes, Jay said that his mom was an artist and his dad worked "in sod," which I thought was a really creative way of describing a small-time drug dealer. The topic of fuzz busters came up. Dad and Jay had the same model.

The moment we finished eating, Dad beat it back to the TV. Mom took our plates. Jay and I couldn't stop smiling at each other. He said his goodbyes and thank-you's, and I walked him outside. I was so relieved. That couldn't have possibly gone any better.

"Really? You think I did a good job?" Jay said.

"You were perfect!"

"Okay. Good. There were a couple times I thought your dad was gonna start beating my ass."

"For what?"

"Anything. You name it."

Just before turning the ignition, Jay closed his eyes, like he always did. The engine turned over. Nas blasted. Jay let out a sigh.

I leaned in and kissed him goodbye—my first time doing so during daylight hours. Walking back to my house, I felt so grown up, like I had taken control of something. From the bushes, I snatched the purple daisy.

Dad clicked through channels. Mom scrubbed the pots.

"Well? What'd you guys think?" I said.

"Seems like a good kid," Dad said. "Get his Social so I can run his credit."

"He's a really nice guy, C.C.," Mom said. "Now, was that so hard, introducing him to your parents?"

Yes, I thought. "No," I said.

I filled a Dixie cup with water, snipped off a bit of the stem, and dropped the daisy inside.

Jay stopped by nearly every night. On the porch, we played Ping-Pong. Best out of five, best out of seven—our games were very competitive. Jay had a fast forehand; I'd say it was his signature shot. But I was like a human wall. Nothing got past me. The only time I lost a point was when my offense got sloppy.

To the rhythmic pock-*pock,* pock-*pock,* Mom swung on the swing. Jay and I let out agonized howls after losing points, and she'd jump a little. Our games were always close in score. When I won, Jay reacted with a short freak-out. He'd hit himself in the head with the paddle, then push me into the pool. "All right, I forgive you," he'd say a moment later, and he'd take off his shirt and jump in. He swam from shallow to deep end in fast, precise strokes, his dark head and body, slippery and sleek like a dolphin, appearing at intervals, luminous under the moon.

Mom and I still went to the mall, but now Jay came with us. His mom never took him shopping for new clothes. Everything he wore was a hand-me-down from his brothers. Jay really didn't mind, but Mom did. "That's how I grew up," she said. She bought him Billabong T-shirts and board shorts, K-Swiss shoes.

After the mall, we'd stop at Sound Splash. A hole-in-the-wall with a spray-painted sign in a strip mall on Okeechobee, Sound Splash was the only place we could get underground music: L7, Tool, banned videos of Marilyn Manson. Graffiti covered the walls: "Neil Young is God." "Jesus was a Rasta." "Cocksucker" scribbled over a picture of Linda Tripp. The pummeling thrash of Fugazi shot from the store's speakers, and I hated walking in with Mom. There was no one over twenty in this place—*ever*. But Mom didn't care. She walked around with her Dooney & Bourke purse, head bopping to the music, so happy to be out and about that I just didn't have the heart to ask her to wait in the car. Plus, Jay wasn't nearly as self-conscious as me. He went about looking at music, and I stayed close to him.

The owner encouraged us to open anything in stock and listen to it. There was even a little station with headphones. "Can I listen to somethin'?" Mom said.

The owner dropped in a PJ Harvey CD and handed her headphones. Surrounded by black-light posters and burning incense, Mom bopped her head along to the beat. "I like this song," she said, loudly, to the owner. Her expression turned coy. "How'd you know I'd like this song?"

The owner tossed up his hands, and I could feel the heat radiating from my face: Mom was flirting. It was happening more and more. At Wendy's, when she ordered a salad and it came with bread, and the guy behind the counter asked if she wanted it toasted or not, "Lemme see this bread," she said, one hand on her hip. "I usually don't like my bread toasted. You like your bread toasted?" On the weekends, Jay and I loved going to Singer Island. Seeing me pack my bag, Mom would hint that she'd like to come along, that a day at the beach sure as hell would beat staying at home. "Sure," I said, forcing a smile. "That sounds fun." I spritzed my hair with Sun In. She plucked her bikini line. Slathered in tanning oil, Mom angled her towel toward guys. Over her workbook version of *Love Yourself, Heal Your Life,* she made eyes, and eventually one of the guys came over and struck up a conversation. Mom giggled and giggled. When we were driving home, the car smelled of coconut suntan lotion. Our sticky, sandy legs stuck to the leather seats, and Mom was so giddy she couldn't talk fast enough. "He lives *on* Singer Island. In a high-rise! Gave me his phone number, told me to call him, we'd go out to dinner some night. And you know what? I'm thinkin' a goin'. Simply because it has been forever since I've gone out with a man who actually showed interest in me."

"You're married," I said from the back seat.

She glanced at me in the rearview mirror. "Yeah. You're right. Oh, shit. Anyway. Still fun to think about."

Jay drove with Mom to my away games. Thinking of him listening to her problems, alone, while going fifty miles per hour in the left lane on I-95, made me feel awful. I told him if he didn't want to do it I'd understand. He assured me that Mom's behavior didn't bother him nearly as much as it bothered me. He thought it was funny. He said a lot of moms were like that. "That's their thing," he said. "They're bored and want to look good for guys."

During warm-ups, I watched from the court as Mom and Jay climbed the bleachers and found seats. By tip-off, Dad would join them, brown-bagged tallboy in hand. They waved at me, gave thumbs up. "Let's go, C.C.!" Suddenly, beneath those hazy yellow gym lights, among the other smiling families, we seemed normal. I don't know. Maybe we were.

I was named Class 4A Player of the Year. *The Palm Beach Post* did a profile on me. They sent a photographer to my school. He situated me into all kinds of different positions and scenarios, each one more embarrassing than the next. The picture that made it onto the front page of the sports section was of me, in color, one hand on my hip and the other tossing a basketball into the air. Looking dead square into the camera lens, I appeared determined. "For the Record," the headline read. Then: "Make that records. Loxahatchee's C.C. Borkoski holds 27 of them. Colleges have started to notice her."

Sometimes recruitment letters arrived at my house, but most of the time they turned up on the corner of the guidance counselor's desk, and I'd get a pink slip saying I needed to pick them up. Flagler College, Georgia Southern, University of North Florida: It made me so incredibly happy to rip open the envelopes, though I never really knew what to make of the letters. Sometimes they were generic, typed with my name inserted in a few places, questionnaires attached to brochures about the school. A few asked me to send updated transcripts, including my ACT and SAT score reports. I had yet to take any standardized tests. They wanted to know: Had I taken any Honors or AP classes? (No.) Was my GPA competitive? (No.) If not, would I consider applying for early decision? I had no idea what they were talking about. But other times, the letters seemed totally *real*. Beneath the U MIAMI BASKET-BALL header was a handwritten letter: "C.C., You are an outstanding basketball player and we believe that you are one of the best point guard prospects in the class of 1999. In order to continue your ascent to the top of our recruiting board, it is critical that you attend our winter camp. Our staff would be thrilled to host you. GO CANES!"

One month later, Mom and Jay dropped me off on campus. Jay made a big deal of it. "C.C.!" he said in pride and astonishment every time we passed a building that looked important. There were so many trees, enormous banyans with swollen branches. The second Jay and I saw the University Green, we bolted from the car and ran to the expansive manicured lawn. People were Hacky Sacking. I couldn't help but do a cartwheel. Jay did some sit-ups and lunges. "Just like I'm in college! Do I look like I'm in college?" he said, with the biggest smile. "Good luck, kid!" Mom said, as we said goodbye. Jay handed me my bag. He whispered in my ear, "I'm gonna get my shit together, I promise."

"Your shit *is* together," I said.

I watched them drive away. Sitting in the passenger seat, Jay ran his fingers through his hair so hard it looked like he was going to peel his own scalp off.

A half-hour later, I was warming up with sixty other girls. They were good, I could tell. Putting backspin on the ball as they threw it onto the court. A waterfall of shots, all long-range jumpers. The head coach watched from the sidelines. I'd seen her on ESPN, and I couldn't quite believe that I was in her presence, that she was now watching *me*. We did strength drills with weights in our hands, on our ankles, elbows, and waists, bands around our ankles. We scrimmaged. Two minutes into the game, I sank my first three-pointer. Minutes later, the girl guarding me swiped the ball from my hands so quickly that I barely had a chance to react. That hadn't happened to me since middle school. I finished with ten points and six assists, but it was okay. My nerves had regulated. I'd do better next scrimmage.

We walked along the brick path, under a natural canopy of hardwood trees. The dorm was so exotic. Plate-glass windows, walls covered with announcements for open poetry slams, study breaks, and opportunity after opportunity to experience selfless devotion to the world and humanity at large. Volunteer at a domestic-violence shelter in Lima, Peru! Help shepherds plant lavender fields in the majestic French Alps! I hadn't realized that was part of being a college student.

From the top floor, I looked out the open dorm window. I swore I could smell the ocean. Everyone looked so happy below me, walking along with their backpacks. They seemed at peace and self-assured. It seemed almost like a sham to think that that could be me one day. I pushed the doubt from my head.

———— **12.** ————

I STARED AT THE SONOGRAM. I didn't understand how it could be a baby. It looked like a galaxy—swirling patterns of light and wispy, luminous clouds marked out against darkness. I slipped the sonogram back into the envelope. Then changed my mind and hung it on the refrigerator.

At first, Lorraine was excited about her pregnancy. She'd call collect from Adena to talk about baby names. Her enthusiasm surprised me. Her due date basically marked the nine-month anniversary of Victor's death. I totally assumed the baby was his, and it seemed depressing to have a child under those circumstances. But Lorraine never mentioned anything about Victor. She had started dating a new guy, Tom Dawg, and said the baby was his.

"Is Mom around? Does she ask how I'm doin'? Can I talk to her?" Lorraine said.

"Hold on." I put the phone on mute. Mom was sitting right there on the couch.

"Do you want to talk to Lorraine? She wants you to ask how she's doing."

"Screw it. Is she askin' me how *I'm* doin'?"

I waited a few more seconds, then unmuted Lorraine. "I can't find her," I said.

The closer Lorraine got to her due date, the more overwhelmed she became—to the point where her voice shook. She swore she wasn't using drugs, but Grandpa threw her out for smoking pot in the house, and she moved in with Tom Dawg. After that, if I spoke to her any time after 7:00 P.M. she was slurring her words. I asked my parents what we would do if the baby didn't come out normal. Dad said there wasn't anything we could do. Mom said God would handle it.

Lorraine gave birth to Desiree. Lorraine didn't mention any abnormalities or problems. She just said she needed help. I assumed we would go to Ohio. Dad did, too. Lorraine called every day, asking if we'd bought our plane tickets. Mom came up with reasons not to go. She said she didn't want me missing school; then the plane tickets were too expensive; and then it was something about us not having winter clothes. "We need to meet our granddaughter, Mary Kay," Dad said. He tossed a credit card onto the counter. It stayed there for months, until, one day, I noticed it was gone.

When I think back on this time, what I most remember is the feeling of being in the dark. In my house, arguments had always been loud. When someone went to jail, we went as a family to bail them out. Diaries and notes were public domain. Doors stayed open or were removed from the hinges altogether. But life as I knew it had slammed shut. What snippets of conversations I overheard, what images I did glimpse, only caused confusion. One morning, before school, I was eating cereal at the kitchen counter when, from the hallway, Mom whispered, "C.C.!"

"What?" I said.

She motioned, *Come here.*

I walked toward her. "What?" I said.

She led me into the master bedroom. I heard the water running. Dad was in the shower. "Keep your eye on the phone," she said.

"Why?"

"Will you just do as I say for once?"

I stared at the see-through plastic, and the neat inner working of wires.

"Mom, wh—"

It flashed pink, the way it always did when a receiver was lifted in another room. Except there was no receiver being lifted in another room.

"See that?" Mom crossed her arms. "What the hell is that thing doin'?"

She had the most serious look on her face. I didn't understand what the big deal was.

"It's old. Throw it away," I said, and returned to my bowl of cereal.

It was my spring break. Mom seemed restless. She flipped through the channels, got up, straightened a pillow. Sat back down. Went to the bathroom, filed her nails. "You know what? To hell with it," she said. "I need a vacation. Let's go to Ohio! Without your father." She clapped her hands.

Mom was not a spontaneous person, so that part was out of character. But I liked that she was suddenly in a good mood. She got out the duffel bags. We started to pack. There was something strange about how quickly this was happening. It felt like we were running away. Or like I was assisting in my own kidnapping. I kept looking at Mom, trying to detect what was going on. She avoided making eye contact. It felt like I should call Dad. Or suggest that we should call Dad. That at the very least he should know we were leaving. I felt like he was going to be upset at us for taking off. I mean, he wanted to meet the baby, too. But I also knew that mentioning the word "Dad" would make Mom mad.

"You wanna ask Jay to come? He can come if he wants," she said.

I wasn't sure I wanted Jay to come. I felt guilty asking him—like I was putting him on the spot. What guy would want to spend his spring break with his girlfriend and her mom and her sister and her sister's baby? But if Jay came along, we'd have to return to Loxahatchee. I wasn't running away or being kidnapped after all. I called him.

"Your mom said it's okay?" he said.

"It was her idea," I said.

Jay got his shifts covered, and when he called back, he sounded excited: "I've never been to Ohio!" Mom said we would pick him up. She didn't want him having to leave his car in the driveway. We set out multiple bowls for Snickers and overfilled them with food. I finally found the courage and asked, "Don't you think we should tell Dad?" Mom waved away my question. "He won't give a shit."

The three of us took turns driving. The interstate was fast and smooth until we hit Wheeling, West Virginia. Then we took beat-up county roads. Barricades and nets were set up to stop boulders from crashing down on top of cars. The bridges were green, rusty, often unusable. It seemed like every time we came upon one we had to detour. The little towns had their traffic lights turned off. They couldn't afford to pay the electricity.

After that, it was hills and valleys. Sharp bends, blind spots, deep descents. Our ears popped. Nothing was level. All the coal had been dug out from beneath the land, which was now reclaimed sludge. There weren't even any cows on it. The only animals we saw were dead deer on the side of the road.

Adena greeted us in its usual way. Its welcome sign consisted of chicken-wire mesh stapled to a pair of two-by-fours. Rusty metal triangles hanging from the chicken wire announced, ADENA LIONS CLUB, ADENA BASEBALL LEAGUE, ST. CASIMIR'S ROSARY SOCIETY, WELCOME TO ADENA: THE TOWN TOO TOUGH TO DIE.

At the sign's base stood a three-foot-high ceramic Virgin Mary, praying in her faded blue cloak. Her hairline remained cracked from when my cousin threw a baseball at her head, on a dare. Her hands were still stained red from when we Sharpied them with stigmata.

Inside my aunt's house, porcelain knickknacks clinked and jingled every time a foot touched the linoleum. The kitchen smelled of powdered sugar. I asked Mom if she was going to come with us to see Desiree. "Maybe later," she said, "I need my coffee first." Then: "When I'm ready to see her, I'll see her." Beneath the aghast expressions of the apostles in the *Last Supper* painting hanging on the wall, Mom and her sisters painted their nails and gave one another perms. To wash out the chemicals, they poured tomato juice over their heads.

It was a forty-minute walk to Lorraine and Tom Dawg's place. Mom wouldn't let us use her car. She said she needed it, in case she wanted to go to Pocketbook Bingo. Every day, the sky was the color of wet newspaper. Every day, it was thirty degrees. Along the two-lane highway, the dirt was loose and steep. Eighteen-wheelers flew past Jay and me. Drivers yelled out their windows for us to get off the road. *And go where?* I wondered. The train tracks we used to walk along to cut through town had been pulled.

"I didn't realize Ohio was like this," Jay said.

"Like what?"

"Hills. I feel like I'm gonna get beat up."

We stopped to admire every abandoned car. Black fungus grew from their shells.

"No Smoking" signs were taped to the windows of the house. Lorraine's two packs a day had obviously gotten on the landlord's nerves. Cigarette butts and burnt matches littered the outdoor carpet that covered the porch. The minute we stepped inside, Tom Dawg would say goodbye and slip out the back door. Lorraine, haggard in her pink, highly flammable nylon nightgown, would hand over Desiree, then disappear. I sat on the couch and held her. She didn't look like Victor. She didn't look like Lorraine or Tom Dawg, either. She didn't look like anyone I had ever met in my life. Her little hands moved constantly, like she was doing a magic trick. Her eyes were bottomless and dark. Not brown. Navy blue? I couldn't tell. They were just dark and locked in on me in what I took to be a plea for help. Lorraine came back in time to watch *Days of Our Lives,* but she couldn't watch it without snorting an Oxy 40. "Especially now that Marlena has amnesia and can't remember who really loves her," she said.

There were no groceries. There was no grocery store. Lorraine got her food from a food bank, and it spoiled and wilted fast. Her refrigerator was covered in mold and pamphlets offering tips on ways to avoid shaking your baby. One pamphlet was headed *People You Can Reach Out To If You Need a Break.* The lines that followed were blank.

Jay hated that he knew so much about babies, but because of his older brothers, he really knew everything there was to know about babies. If it weren't for him, I don't know what I would've done. When Desiree thrashed and cried, Jay took her into the bathroom, shut the door, and turned the hair dryer on low. He poured some kind of cereal into her bottle and mixed it with milk and water. After her bath, we let her crawl naked. Jay said it would help dry out her diaper rash. When that didn't work, Jay said it wasn't diaper rash. He looked closer at her butt. "Dust mites," he said. I got mad at Lorraine: "You need to keep the house clean!"

"No shit, dude. How many times do I have to say it? I need help."

We mopped. We washed everything—curtains, stuffed animals, pillows—in hot water, and I put Desiree to sleep in her fresh bed. As I watched her breathe hard, my heart swelled so tight from love and worry that I thought I was having a panic attack.

Lorraine wanted to go to West Virginia (where cigarettes were cheaper), then to County to try to get pills. I wanted to stop somewhere and get clothes and diapers for Desiree. We piled into the car—a rusted-out twenty-year-old Pinto that Lorraine had bought for three hundred dollars. The roof's interior lining drooped so low that it rested on top of our heads. There was no heat, baby seat, or back-seat floorboards. I sat Indian-style and held Desiree over my shoulder. I didn't think it was a big deal until Lorraine started flying along those winding roads and I saw the pavement rushing beneath us. Each time Desiree wiggled, my palms grew more sweaty, and I imagined dropping her and watching her *POP!* like a water balloon and disappear beneath the car. There was no shoulder, no way for Lorraine to stop or turn around. Tiny pieces of gravel kicked up from the road. They *tinged!* off the windows and ricocheted off my face. Jay kept looking back at me: "You okay? You okay?" I couldn't talk. If I opened my mouth, a piece of gravel would chip my tooth. Or I'd puke. No wonder Desiree was such a serious baby. She had no choice but to be.

Shell-shocked, exhausted, Jay and I waited for Tom Dawg to come home. We watched the local news. The crimes were similar to the crimes in Florida (man shoots wife). But in Florida, the criminals ran, or engaged in a shootout with the police. Here, they called the cops on themselves and waited, hands up, on the porch.

Tom Dawg arrived and it was confusing. He said he'd only made seven bucks and that nobody had come in today. But when I asked him where he worked, he said he didn't have a job.

"So where did you make seven bucks?" I said.

"Remanufacturing computer ink cartridges."

"So you do have a job," I said.

"Nah. You know what I'm sayin'?"

" 'Ink cartridge' is code for something?" I said.

He laughed. He didn't seem like a bad guy. He just wasn't all there.

"Of course he's not. How can he be? He's with your sister," Mom said, eating popcorn, playing Aces with her sisters. I mentioned how Lorraine didn't wake up when Desiree cried. How their phone was turned off. How her bathroom walls were buckled.

"Think I don't know what poverty looks like?" Mom said. "Why do you think we got the hell outta here?"

I thought my aunts would be insulted by what my mother was saying. After all, this was their home; it was where they'd raised their children. But they nodded along in agreement. Aunt Cookie said if I was that concerned for Desiree's safety I could file a report. "No one likes to do it, but if you think it's necessary," she said. Aunt Sissy and Aunt Connie got mad at her for putting the idea in my head. "Just 'cause your sister's a drug addict doesn't mean she's a terrible mother," Aunt Sissy said.

"That's exactly why she's a terrible mother," I said.

"As long as she doesn't die, that baby'll be fine," Aunt Connie said. "You don't want her going into foster care. She won't have a shot in hell."

Aunt Sissy sighed. "I don't know. Some people are doomed from the start," she said, and I didn't know who she was talking about: Lorraine or Desiree.

"Just leave it be, C.C.," Mom said. "Your sister'll figure it out. We all did." She reminded Jay and me that we were on vacation. Shouldn't we have some fun?

Because my great-great-uncle Adolph fought against the Nazis in World War II, we only had to pay twenty-five cents for a Budweiser draft at the Legion. The red lights made lit cigarettes burn gold and jars of pickled pigs' feet glow pink. Handmade posters glittered. "To Our Hero Desert Foxes! Tina, Melissa, Heather, Yvonne!" At the long bar, guys just a few years older than Jay and me took turns on the portable phone, trying to get in touch with their girlfriends in Iraq.

I wanted to talk to Jay; I wanted to ask if he thought it was weird that my mom had come all this way to *not* see the baby. But he seemed distracted. Or more like he was pretending to be distracted. I could tell he didn't want to be bombarded with any more of my family's drama. I should've listened to my instincts; I should never've invited him. He'd wasted his whole spring break on *this*. I felt guilty. I wanted to lighten the mood, laugh, stroke his dick beneath the bar, but my worrying made me feel unsexy. So did the pigs' feet.

"I love you," I said. I rested my head on his shoulder.

"I love you, too." He didn't kiss my hair like he usually did.

I didn't file a report. Mom never did meet Desiree. We drove back to Florida. Mom talked and talked the entire drive, her voice ranging from strong to soft. Jay and I weren't part of the conversation. We looked out the windows. We pretended to sleep. I don't think Mom even noticed. Or, if she did, she didn't mind. She talked until she ran out of words. "I don't know," she said, as though we had asked a question, "I don't know nothin'." We dropped Jay off at his house. As always, he thanked my mom profusely for all the things she had paid for: The food at the rest stop. The gas. The tolls. Mom made sure he got into his house okay. I climbed into the front seat.

"I don't think your father needs to know that Jay came along. Let's just keep that between us," Mom said.

It was such an odd request—I couldn't remember a time when she had asked me to keep a secret—that the *why* of it didn't cross my mind. All I could think was that Jay had just spent a week with our relatives. *Of course* it would get back to Dad.

"You're a good kid," Mom said, "you know that?"

Days later, I was sitting in front of my stereo, listening to music, when Dad came into my room—which is something he never did. He was wearing his work clothes and holding a paper grocery bag adorned with a green hurricane grid. His expression was serious. *Lorraine killed Desiree,* I thought.

"Pumpkin, you know I love you, right?" His manner was terse. Like he was holding back. Or holding something in.

"I know," I said.

He pulled from his pocket a tape and dropped it into the cassette player. He pushed "play."

Static. Then the dialing of a touch-tone phone. Long-belled rings hummed through the air. Dad fast-forwarded.

"What are you doing?" I said. Outside my room, Mom shuffled around the kitchen. Cupboards opened, closed. Dad pushed "play."

"Troy Crumbley, Ma'am, with the Council of Firefighters."

"I'm not in a very good mood," Mom said.

"I got somethin' that'll cheer ya up. We're taking pre-orders for our Palm Beach County firefighter calendar!"

Dad hit the fast-forward button, harder this time. He pushed "play."

"I'm so excited! We'll have so much fun! I'll try to skip last period."

It was me. I didn't like this. I pushed "stop."

"Pumpkin," Dad said.

"What?"

"Your mother's screwin' your boyfriend."

The boundaries of my body vanished. I felt enormous and as expansive as air. I dissolved into the walls, the carpet, my father.

"Dinner!" Mom yelled.

Dad dropped the paper bag on my bed and hurried out. I opened it. There were more tapes, dozens of them. I shoved it beneath my bed.

Feeling shaky, I walked into the kitchen. Mom had on her lobster-claw oven mitts. Dad filled his glass with ice. "I got some bad news," he said.

Oh no. I opened the silverware drawer.

"We hit two numbers on the lotto and that was it. We didn't even get a payoff."

"Maybe next time," I said, baffled, but going along with it. I pulled out forks, no knives.

We sat down to eat. Mom said grace. Dad gave her a nudge. "Pass the bread and butter, will ya, hon?"

13

I STOOD ON THE DECK of the *Kingsbury* as it hopped choppy waters. Six miles off the coast of Maine, the landscape was austere. Barren rocks heaped together. Mountains of scrap metal. Mountains of salt. We docked on the rocky edge of Appledore Island. We were greeted by others from the Our Irreplaceable Home conservation conference. They held long, skinny sticks. One woman was older, in her fifties, and wore a satiny suit recycled from plastic bottles. She handed me a stick. "Don't be afraid to use it. They're vicious," she said. We looked up at the gulls swarming low.

Showing me to the dorm, she talked a little about her work as a glacial archaeologist. She believed the bubonic plague was trapped in Siberian ice. "It's thawing. It's astonishing, the mayhem and old secrets emerging."

I been feelin' low. I went to the beach today. By myself, of course. Money doesn't matter. I just wanna be happy. I need a husband I can talk to. All these years, I been so alone with Cal. When is it gonna end? I'm tired of not being a partner with somebody. Goddamnit. This phone's been actin' funny. You hear that clickin'?

I was at the conference to learn new ways of inspiring sustainability. My boss was reframing our mission statement so that it completely centered on climate change. But in rewriting our signage, pamphlets, and zookeeper talks, I was struggling. There was a play between emotion and logic, the affirmation and negation of ecological reality, that I just couldn't hit on. I needed to communicate more hope. The higher-ups at Ardsley were getting impatient with me. "Under no circumstance, C.C., can a visit to our zoo leave guests questioning whether they want to have children."

The conference was connected to Shoals Marine Laboratory. Inside wood-paneled classrooms, doors opened to the squawk of seagulls and to the breeze and smell of the ocean. I befriended activists, professors, behaviorists, and ecotourism travel guides. We attended lectures on plastics, petroleum, and nutrient pollution. Beside our desks, bubbling tanks of ocean water kept sea creatures alive and well. Long pink tentacles pressed against the glass.

I had periodontal work done today. They stuck something over my head. It was like a View Master with earphones. It had a volume control and a rewind. In front of my eyes, I saw SpongeBob! It was the neatest thing I ever seen in my life!

In the evenings, I ate seaweed salad in the cafeteria with other conference attendees. Industry leaders from Phospholutions spoke at length about algae remediation. A marine biologist clicked through slides of seawater. "Sludge. . . . Invasive snails. . . . Harmful bacteria. . . ."

Cocktail hour was lethargic. We were going to have to buy land in Detroit and eat dirt while awaiting our heat death. A climate-grief specialist tried to explain the difficulty of getting the public to take any real action. "The more something deteriorates, the more likely we are to put it off to the side. Earth included. That's human nature."

I took a look at Calvis today and thought, What the hell did I ever see in him? There ain't a goddamn thing about him that I like. Nothin'! Not one thing. Not even his money. I don't think I been attracted to him for twenty years.

In the sinking sun ablaze in scarlet over the black clay rocks, I scrambled, stick in hand, poking away the gulls. Inside my dorm, I worked on the paper I was set to present: "Acquired from the Wild: Considerations When Choosing the Parents of the Next Generation of the Animal Kingdom."

I poured an enormous glass of whiskey and started to write:

A large portion of conservation work focuses on animals that live in the wild, but captive animal populations are also important for saving species. In the zoo world, a big portion of our energy goes to managing efforts for many endangered and vulnerable animals. Maintaining healthy captive populations is critical in reducing the issues that caused the species numbers to decline in the first place. If the zoo's goal is to reintroduce captive animals into the wild, the most important factor is to choose the best parents we can for our future animal children.

However! A large portion of these animals do have mental deficiencies. And just like in the human world, mentally deficient animals are quite good at hiding their limitations. What to an average zoo visitor looks like restlessness or even boredom looks to zoo staff like ire or a possible neurodegenerative disease. Beauty helps. Your average person will find it very hard to look at a svelte puma, or supple leopard, and think that it may be grappling with a low IQ.

C.C.?

Mom? Hello?

Hi.

Hi. I need a ride home from practice. It ended early. Can you pick me up?

No.

What are you doing?

Nothing.

Nothing?

Nothing. *What are you doin'?*

Why are you laughing?

Nothing.

Mom, what's wrong with you?

I got company here now. What do you need?

Sorry. Who is it?

Why? What do you want me to do?

Pick me up from practice. Who's at the house?

The girl down the street.

Who?

The girl that lives in the house down the street.
You don't know her name?
I can't remember her name.
And she's over at the house?
Yeah. She's right here.
Mom, you're freaking me out. You're acting weird.
I'm actin' weird? Well, I am weird. You know me.
I finished my whiskey and poured myself another one.

Parents are mirrors, reflecting back to their children who they are and who they will be. If a father peacock is charismatic, bold, and strong, its offspring will believe they have that inner strength as well. If a mother cougar is pitiful or juvenile, her offspring will believe that they are, too. No matter where children find themselves in life, it is nearly impossible for them to see a path that is different from their parents'. They *are* the path.

One of the first lessons I learned from working at the zoo had to do with understanding animals' emotions. They, like humans, experience an array of them. Seeing animal emotion—joy, sorrow, jealousy—allows us to recognize ourselves, which is why animals are so powerful: they evoke our empathy. It's why anthropomorphizing is an easy, effective form of storytelling, especially at zoos. It's also something you have to resist. When humans ascribe emotions to other animals, they imagine those emotions to be the same as theirs. They aren't, and they can't be. Animals' sensory apparatuses are different from ours, so their experience and their awareness of the world are different from ours, too. The more we view animals as humans, the more likely we are to let our guard down in their presence. This is why chimpanzees in board shorts rip off women's faces.

I don't want you picking my son up from school, Mary Kay. It's happened multiple times now. If Jay's not feeling well, he can call me.
Since when do you take care of your kid?

In the wood-paneled classroom, I stood behind the podium and looked out to the audience. "I'm not saying that attempting to emotionally understand an animal is bad, or even impossible. I'm just saying that, no matter how close you feel to your pet snake, never, ever, put it around your neck."

I smiled to the small, polite applause.

The head climatologist was next. She told us about how much of her life had been focused on the ocean, how much she had tried to help, and how she was met at every turn with legislative and environmental restrictions preventing her from making lasting change. She spoke about how devastated she was to be leaving the next generation with a natural world that was worse than the one she had inherited. "It's now best to view oceans as graveyards and vacations as once-in-a-lifetime opportunities," she said. "Not because we won't be able to return to the places we visit, but when we do, the landscape will be unrecognizable."

Piles of snow blocked the windows, darkening the gloomy apartment. Dinner reservations were for seven o'clock. Alex got dressed and I sat on the bed. After three years of marriage, and three months of pretending everything was normal, he was ready to tell his parents the truth: we were getting divorced.

For Alex, this was the ultimate failure; he'd be the first in his family to go through one. "First journalism. Now this," he said.

He had lost weight. Underneath his tailored suit there was a frailty to him. He had shingles. The doctor said it was common: marital stress will do that, even to a thirty-year-old.

Alex said he was willing to do whatever it took to stay married. I wasn't. To admit that out loud made me feel selfish, but it was the truth. With each passing day, with each friend's baby announcement, with each Darien dinner party and news that another family friend had cloned their dog, with each holiday card the Wellmans sent out detailing everyone's accomplishments, and the professional photograph they'd tuck inside of all of us, dressed up, on Compo Beach, them smiling so genuinely and lovingly and me off to the side looking, or at least feeling, like some rugged bacterium accidentally released into their environment via ballast water, I felt the creeping awareness that I was not going to be able to adapt to this life. And all the little dramas of resisting or adjusting to its pressures were wearing me down. Alex had gotten laid off at the *Hartford Courant,* and it was the most exciting time in our marriage. He'd wake up late and drink his coffee, and we'd have sex against the built-in ironing board. Then he'd go online and look for jobs. There were so many possibilities. Maybe he'd work at *The New York Times,* and I could work at the Bronx Zoo. Or maybe he'd get a job at the *Miami Herald* and we could live in one of those cool bungalows outside Coral Gables. But that's not what happened. He went to work for his father. I understood that it was a stable, high-paying job, and that he was lucky to have it, but the seamlessness with which Alex turned into a businessman was shocking. He traded in his Saab 900, which I loved with all my heart, for a Mercedes E-Class Coupe. Dressed in a suit and tie, he drove to his father's office park in Stratford, where he oversaw the building of a new outlet mall. He talked a lot about elevators, and I didn't understand: how did he know so much about elevators?

I once asked Alex what it meant to be elite.

"Who's using the word?" he said.

"Someone who makes under fifty thousand a year."

"When the lower classes use the word 'elite,' that's another way of saying they resent you for having achieved something that makes your life better," he said.

That didn't seem right to me. I thought the lower classes considered the elite to be made up of people who didn't so much achieve as inherit. Which was much different. And that's how I came to view Alex. It made it hard for me to respect him.

The way I saw it, if I left Alex, I would lose the only person on this earth who offered me love and safety. The only person who made me smarter. Without him, my emergency contact on every work application would be 911, and I'd basically go back to being dumb. But if I stayed with him, I would live in a world where I would never belong and that I didn't necessarily like. Loss was inevitable either way. But how could Alex and I ever fully understand each other? We couldn't accept even what we *could* understand about each other.

Alex wanted me to accompany him to dinner. He thought

it would be more respectful if we broke the news together to his parents. I thought my presence would make things awkward. I imagined the Wellmans pressuring us to give it more time, to seek counseling, which they'd be happy to pay for. It took a lot of energy to stand up to their goodwill, and I knew from experience I couldn't count on Alex to help me with that. Which would leave me sitting there, picking at my striped bass, feeling like an *unthankful skank* (said my sister's voice in my head).

"You're not confessing a crime, Alex. Nobody died. You'll feel better once you get it over with."

He put on his coat. I handed him his gloves. "Will you do something for me?" I said. He didn't answer. "When you tell them, can you record it on your phone?"

"C.C., I am not your father."

"Okay." He looked mad. "I'm sorry."

"He really warped how you relate to people. You know that, right?"

"I want to know what they think. I mean, I suspect some things, but . . ."

"If you want to know how people truly feel about you, why don't you earn their trust and ask them?"

"You're right. I'm sorry. Pl—"

He walked out. Shamefaced, I went straight to the liquor store and bought an enormous bottle of Jack, the kind with the handle, so we could drink it when he got home.

Three hours later, I heard his key in the door. I poured us glasses, big ones.

"How'd it go?" I said.

He loosened his tie and sat down. He looked tired. He pulled his phone from his pocket. "I recorded it," he said.

I sat beside him. "Oh my gosh. Why? You didn't have to. We don't have to listen to it."

"I like bending the rules, too," he said to the table.

Being sad made him look extra handsome. I was so touched and surprised by what he had done that I considered getting back with him right then and there. I moved my chair closer. He tapped "play." The *ting!* of a spoon stirring coffee came across clear. Alex cleared his throat.

"*I have to tell you something. C.C.'s not here tonight because we're getting divorced.*"

An "*Oh no.*" Mr. Wellman said, "*I'm sorry, son.*" Mrs. Wellman asked, "*Why?*"

"*We have a lot of problems. She doesn't understand the value, the benefits, of staying together.*"

I cringed. It made me sound as loving and open-minded as a jackhammer.

"*Have you gone to therapy?*"

"*No.*"

"*Do you want to go to therapy?*"

"*I do. She doesn't.*"

A long stretch of silence. Finally, Mrs. Wellman spoke: "*Alex, when you're on your high horse, you are insufferable. But that does not impugn your character. I really think she's doing the wrong thing. She'll regret it. With all the crises that go on in her family, you'd think she'd want stability, not shy away from it. She has no idea how alone she'll be.*"

"*Baked Alaska?*"

"*Oh. Here. Thank you.*"

"*More cappuccino?*"

"*Yes. Thank you.*"

God. This was like a modern, audio rendition of *Our*

Town. I felt the carpe-diem theme strongly: Appreciate the small things, spend time with your loved ones, enjoy the expensive dessert. Because, when you die, it'll make you sick that you didn't appreciate it more. So sick that you won't even want to be a ghost. It'll be too painful to be reminded of what you left behind.

The recording muffled, then stopped.

Alex traced the bridge of his nose and looked at me. "You can't get to the trust. It's protected. You know that, right?"

"I don't want your money, Alex." The words were hard to say. I felt insulted. And misunderstood. I saved money (and the environment) by using rainwater and a hand-crank wringer to wash our socks and underwear. I flushed the toilet as little as possible, to the point that Alex complained about the bathroom smelling like an aquarium. Now, suddenly, I was going to find a way to "get to the trust"? So I could do what, buy a Louis Vuitton?

"Not a Louis Vuitton," he said. "I figured . . ."

"You figured what?"

"It's not like we have any assets."

"I understand that."

He leaned back in the chair. "Where are you going to live? How are you going to support yourself?"

"I know how to support myself. I'll live here. Unless you wanna live here."

"I'd prefer to stay here while I look for a place to buy."

"Let's flip for it." I grabbed my purse, looked for a quarter.

"You can't afford the full rent here and your bills."

"I'll get a second job," I said.

"Uh-huh. Where?"

"Seven-Eleven. Alex, why all the aggression and mistrust?"

"Why should I trust you?"

"What do you need to trust me *for*? Isn't that why I signed the prenup? So you didn't have to trust me? What do we own? The dresser? You can have it."

"C.C., did you ever love me?"

"Yes," I said. "I still do. Just not enough."

I set the quarter on my thumb. "Call it."

On the day I was set to move out, Alex helped me pack my books into boxes. He presented me with a gift: a gray Osprey hiking backpack from REI. "I don't want you lugging your shit around in garbage bags," he said.

I tried it on. The hip belt fit perfectly. "I love it," I said. We rolled my clothes and stuffed them inside. "Do you wanna have sex one last time?" I said.

"No," he said.

One last walk-through, and I grabbed the wine opener, the Italian coffeepot, and my Free People coat. "You need a towel?" he said, and I nodded. I looked under the bed, just like you do before checking out of a hotel.

It felt too depressing for Alex to walk me to my car, so I asked if we could say goodbye in the hallway. After a whole marriage, after everything that he'd given me, or wanted or tried to give me, I wanted to say something loving. But the sentences that popped into my head sounded trite, or like I was making them up.

"Thank you," I said. I meant it. It felt convincing.

"At least try to consolidate your federal loans," he said, and opened the door.

14.

EVEN AS AN ADULT, I have no idea if what I experienced is rare or if it happens a lot and people are too ashamed to talk about it. Whenever I googled "My mom had sex with my boyfriend," all that came up was porn.

Then, one night, around the time I married Alex, I came across a Reddit thread: "I [F17] just found out that my boyfriend [M17] is sleeping with my mom [F48]."

I approached the post skeptically—I had the feeling it was some horny high-school kid making shit up. But by the end, I was certain that [F17] was telling the truth. What she most wanted to know—her whole reason for sharing her story—was: "Should I confront them?" Which was the question I most struggled with when it happened to me.

I scrolled through the Reddit replies. The first one—

"Jer-ry! Jer-ry! Jer-ry!"—received hundreds of upvotes. The classism, so fucking blatant, pissed me off.

"Is this real?"

"Why are you acting normal?"

"Are you financially stable? Can you get out of there?"

"Are you sure? Is your mother really this type of person?"

"Where's your father?"

I knew that these were the exact questions [F17] was asking herself, and I had all the answers. After years of lurking on Reddit, I finally set up an account. In bed, in the dark, phone glow in my face, I told [F17] exactly what to expect.

In the immediate aftermath, most everything took place inside. My body, my mind, the house. Outwardly, I stopped reacting. No matter what I witnessed, what dawned on me, or what was said to me, no matter what dilemma I faced, my expression remained placid. My nervous system, though, existed on high alert—an animal running fast through a quivering forest, subsisting purely on vibration. The little voice inside me still spoke, but only in short, clipped words. *Wait. Don't. Now.*

After I listened to the tapes, I feared that my mother would find them beneath my bed. I feared her knowing that I knew. It was her wrong, but it was humiliating to *me*. I wrapped them in a beach towel and buried them with the Christmas decorations in the attic. In terrible anticipation, I waited for my father to confront my mother. He never did.

The house felt like it was laced with trip wires. One wrong move and I would get electrocuted. Or the roof would blow sky-high. Still, I was afraid to leave the house. I was afraid I'd come home and find Mom or Dad or both of them dead.

My mother was still living in my room. In the mornings,

when she woke up, I pinched my eyes closed and burrowed deep in the sheets. I did a lot of pretending to sleep. It was a major survival mechanism.

One morning, early on, I passed her in the kitchen. She stared uncomprehendingly at the bare counter space. "Where the heck is it?" she said. She opened and closed the microwave, the oven, the dishwasher. "I lost my coffeepot."

She glanced around the kitchen. She could've sworn she'd cleaned it the night before. Mom was a pot-a-day coffee drinker. Without that first sip . . .

"You see my coffeepot?" she said.

I shook my head.

"Where the hell is it? Coffeepots don't just up and disappear."

I went to school, but I don't recall staying there. I started tasks and left them unfinished. I drew baths and didn't get into them. At night, I went to bed early. This is when I dwelled and spiraled and thought about Jay. There was no anger, no sense of betrayal whatsoever. I worried for him as though he were a comrade who had maybe gotten blown up in the air strike. If I could see him, and talk to him, we could figure out a plan. We could come up with a story, a lie, that would help us both. Every night, I thought maybe he would knock on my window. He never did. Each time the phone rang, I thought maybe it was him. It never was.

My feeling was that he knew that I knew, and he was ashamed. Why else would he just drop me? When the urge to reach out to Jay was particularly strong, I went into the bathroom, locked the door, lay on the floor, and did things that allowed me to fixate and release. I masturbated. I felt around my head for wiry pieces of hair, plucked them out at the root,

and tied them into tiny knots. I lived out scenarios and practiced monologues in my head. Imagining myself confronting
Jay, I'd see myself crying. But I wasn't a crier. And the one
sentence that came to mind—*How could you do this to me?*—
felt unnatural and melodramatic. Like something an actress
would say, not me. So in my head I edited it down—*How
could you do this? How could you? How?*—until all the
words were gone. I thought about a childhood memory of
Jay's that he once shared with me. He was seven years old and
his mom took him and his brothers to IHOP, which was a
treat; they never went out to eat. The breakfast was chaotic
with all the kids yelling and punching one another, while all
the while Jay kept ordering glasses of orange juice. He assumed refills were free, but they weren't. The bill arrived and
it was more expensive than the mom had anticipated; she
didn't have enough money to pay it. She and his brothers got
mad at Jay: "How can you be so stupid? What are we gonna
do now?" That's how I kept picturing Jay—as that little boy,
hiding behind an empty orange juice glass, feeling embarrassed, dumb, and alone. And that's how I felt, too. But it
wasn't just a feeling; it was the truth: I was him. He was me.

One afternoon, Dad walked through the house, golf bag
over his shoulder. He sat on the couch, right next to Mom,
and polished his irons with a damp dishcloth. This was it, I
thought. He was going to Jay's golf course. He was going to
beat him up. I kept glancing at Mom for a reaction.

"Ya want me to take the pork chops outta the freezer,
Cal?"

"I'm gonna go hit some balls," he said.

I followed Dad to the front door. I watched him reverse
out of the driveway. For the next two hours, I lay on the tiles,

imagining the violence between Dad and Jay. The front door slammed, and I shot out of the bathroom. Dad's big, drunk smile, and how talkative he was about what a great time he'd had at the range, made me realize he was playing a game. He wanted Mom and me to *believe* he had gone to Jay's work. He *wanted* us to worry. I wondered what he was getting by creating the illusion.

I got called out of Language Arts III. Walking down the portable steps, overgrown with weeds, I was certain my father had shot my mother and then himself. I wondered who was going to break it to me. I wondered how I would react. In the bleached-out concrete walkway, I turned the corner. There was Mom, fresh lipstick, with Dad. They were dressed up.

"Hey, kid," Dad said. "Got a surprise for ya."

I looked to Mom. She held up her palms and smiled.

"Beautiful day out! Ain't it, Pumpkin?" In the rearview mirror, he gave me a wink. Mom bopped her head to the song on the radio. I felt like I was gonna puke; sweat trickled down my arm, and I cracked the window. We pulled into the dealership. NOW YOU'RE TALKING! LES RUSSO FORD! read the enormous banner hanging over the entrance.

Mom and I tagged behind as Dad walked through the showroom, making a nice glide of it. Receptionists in low-cut dresses tied strings to balloons. They looked at us funny. I smiled out of politeness. Mom did, too. Dad poked his head into the sales offices.

"My deal get bought?" he said. He snatched a pair of keys out of midair.

Dad placed his hand around my neck and steered me to the centerpiece of the showroom: a Mustang GT 5.0 hardtop,

black with a red stripe. Off its finish, the overhead lights reflected like tiny stars. "It's all yours, Pumpkin."

I looked to my mother. At first, her face seemed pleased.
Then it dropped.

"I thought we were here to get me a car," she said.

"I traded in your car," Dad said. He opened the door. The
leather, masculine new-car smell hit me as hard as gunmetal.

"You took my car?" Mom said.

"Yep!" Dad said.

"You just took it? You didn't ask me?" Mom said.

"Nope!"

"So . . . she doesn't have a car?" I said, quietly.

"Don't worry about your mother. Get in," Dad said.

I felt guilt, nerves, dread. This was the ultimate "taking
sides." Either I stood up for my mother—she was the adult; it
wasn't right for me to have a car and her not to—or I slid into
the driver's seat and joined Dad's party. No matter which I
chose, things were not going to turn out well; I knew it.

"She doesn't need a car with that much pickup. She's
gonna kill herself," Mom said.

"Feel it out, kid. Car's sharp!" Dad said.

I slid into the driver's seat. The leather was cool on my skin.

"That car belonged to me," Mom said.

"It was a C-O-P," Dad said.

"What the hell is that?"

"A dime and advantage."

"What's that mean?"

"There's a balloon at the end."

"What the hell is a fuckin' balloon, Cal? Sounds like some
asshole name of some asshole car-salesman plan."

Dad laughed so hard he snorted. Salesmen gathered to eavesdrop.

"Let's get two cheaper cars for the price of this one," I said.

Dad squatted down, eye-level. "You're a kid. You don't know what's best for you. I do."

Dad screwed on the license plate. The salesmen pushed open the sliding glass showroom door. I started the ignition, and my mother looked at me. I recognized the expression on her face: furious self-pity. The same look she had when Dad called to say he'd be home late, and when Lorraine attacked her with the cruelest of words. The livid, insecure expression screamed, "I do not deserve this," and I did something I never thought I'd do in real life: I drove right off the showroom floor, tires slipping and squealing on the shiny, white tile.

After that, my mother's face turned—and remained—a light shade of green. A permanent cold sweat shined on her forehead and down the sides of her nose. Whenever she started to speak, she collapsed a little. The only way she could make it through a sentence was if she was sitting. I didn't touch her or hug her or tell her it was going to be okay. Not because I was mad at her, but because I was scared. I stood close, but not too close, and listened.

"Your father is out for himself."

"Your father is stirring up shit."

"What the hell is he up to now?"

"Your father has the morals of a snake."

Dad removed food from the cupboards—oatmeal, boxes of pasta, Cinnamon Toast Crunch, Jif, honey. He tossed it into a box and left it on the front seat of his locked car, along with the coffeepot. Mom could see it through the windows on her way to get the mail. I thought that he was preparing to leave us, that he was moving somewhere and taking that stuff with him. But he kept returning home from work.

We started to run low on groceries. Mom asked me to take her to the store. Driving to Publix with Mom in the passenger seat of my 5.0, engine purring, felt unnatural. It was official: The child had usurped the role of the parent. The animal kingdom was upside down. I didn't know what to do with my power. Own it? Release it? Ask her if she wanted to drive? "Slow down," she said. "Slow down, will you?" I tried to go the speed limit, but I couldn't. She was right. The car had a lot of pickup.

Something about being together, outside of the house, felt dangerous. Like we had been tricked into leaving the cave. I think Mom felt it too. We hurried down the aisles, tossed food into the cart.

"You okay?" said the girl at checkout.

"Shitty day," Mom said. She handed her a credit card.

Declined, I'm sorry. Did she have any cash? No. Not enough. Did she have another card? No. Wait. She did. She did! The Visa Gold Capital One. She pulled it from her wallet. DECLINED.

On the pay phone out front, Mom called the number on the back of the credit card. "My husband. He did this. I have never worked. I have never had a job. And he has used this credit card also. I mean, he has used it, period. It's a joint credit card. He must've canceled it, right? He had to. Is that something someone can just *do*?"

On the car ride home, she looked out the window. "He's gonna burn the house down. I can feel it."

Dad covered the thermostat with a plastic lockbox to

which only he had the key. The house got hot. Comfort, car, access to food, credit cards, everything Mom relied on Dad for, he took away. In the kitchen, he spoke to her calmly and directly. He told her that if she needed money she was to come to him and ask for it. I watched her do just that. He didn't give her cash. He wrote her checks, sometimes post-dated, and never for more than ten dollars. On the memo line, he wrote "FOOD ONLY."

Getting into bed, Mom asked me: "Does that mean I can't buy toilet paper? Or hair spray?" She looked devastated.

"He's bullying you. Cash the check and buy whatever you want."

"But what if the bank finds out I used the money for stuff that wasn't food?"

"The bank doesn't care how you spend the money."

She looked unconvinced. "I don't need them cancelin' this check, C.C. Or askin' for their money back."

"Mom!"

She jumped.

"How will the bank ever *fucking* know what you spent your ten dollars on?"

Her ignorance was pitiful and often frustrating, yet I usually caught myself before lashing out. It made me feel monstrous. Which is why I didn't confront her about Jay. What was in it for me? She was a victim, and under no circumstance would she be denied her victimhood. That was rule number one. Nothing—no matter what I said, felt, did, or didn't do—would *ever* change that.

Curled up on her side of the bed, in her lavender cotton nightgown, she looked so small, like she was never supposed to be anything more than a child.

"I can start sleepin' in the garage if you want," she said.

I turned off the light.

It was on impulse, really, that I decided to drive past Jay's work. I didn't think he would notice me in my new car. It was 3:00 P.M.—the beginning of his shift. Pulling into the employee parking area, nestled in the pines, I glimpsed his red Integra. Every emotion inside me fired at once: fear, sadness, anger, even happiness (*He's here!*). His driver's-side door was open, and he was sitting in the seat. Pulling forward, I took deep breaths and navigated the lot.

My connection to Jay had always been tied up in shame. There'd been so much of it in our lives; that's why I'd been hesitant to confront or even speak with him. The urge was there, but I couldn't bear the thought of bringing up his wrongness—that he had fucked up or disgusted me or even that he had hurt me. There was something about looking him in the eye and forcing him to contend with his bad behavior that made *me* feel like shit. What would I be doing, really, but adding to his shame?

I made sure not to look Jay's way as I passed him on my right. Only when I pulled out of the loop was I able to see all of him in my rearview mirror, staring straight ahead into the deep green woods, shaking a bottle of Yoo-hoo.

The Reddit users came down hard on [F17]'s boyfriend. But in terms of the mother, they showed compassion and tenderness. I was taken aback by their wisdom.

"For you to move forward and live a healthy life, you will have to forgive your mother."

"Many people will say to cut your mom out of your life,

but that is easier said than done. We are biologically pro-
grammed to love Mother."

"Your mom is your mom. There is no excuse, but she is
your mom."

"Forgiving her will lessen your pain. Estrangement causes
cancer."

"My guess is that your mom has been a problem for years
now. This kind of thing can't just happen in a vacuum. Work
hard to maintain some semblance of a relationship with her.
It will be worth it."

They were right. Everything they said was dead-on. There
was only one problem. They were assuming that the mother
wanted a relationship with the daughter. They were assuming
that she *wanted* to be forgiven.

I stayed up late, watching Pac-10 games on ESPN, waiting
for Dad to come home. He walked in the door. I followed him
into the garage. We stood beneath the hard white overhead
light, with the shadows of bugs trapped inside.

"Dad, tell me what's going on."

He opened a drawer on his tool chest and pulled out a new
cassette tape. He tore off the cellophane with his teeth.

"You talk to your mother?"

"I don't wanna talk to her. You talk to her."

"Don't need to."

He shoved the tape into a recorder that I swear he pulled
right out of the exposed insulation on the garage walls. He
was still tapping the phone lines. I hadn't realized that.

"Are you gonna get divorced?"

"I'll go bankrupt before I pay her a dime."

"How long does it take to go bankrupt?"

15.

I WAS ASHAMED. I ASSUMED my parents were, too. It didn't even cross my mind that they would tell other people. Why would they? My mother could get arrested. If there was such a thing as the secret you take to the grave, this was it, I was certain.

Dad told the salesmen at work. They sympathized with him. He was the victim, for once. He asked his GM to fire him: his first step in manipulating the system and preparing himself, financially, for divorce. The GM said of course. Dad had been a terrific asset to the dealership; it was the least he could do. The papers were delivered. Reason for termination: Les Russo Ford is headed in a new direction. Calvis Borkoski is no longer needed. Dad applied for unemployment. He drained his 401(k).

My mother gathered her ten dollars' worth of groceries,

along with what food remained in the far back of the cupboards and freezer. She piled it into the red wagon I'd used to drag my Cabbage Patch Kids around in when I was little. From my bedroom window, I watched her pull it down the street and up our neighbors' driveways. In terry-cloth shorts, with drawstring bows cinched on either side, she knocked on doors. Most neighbors didn't answer, but a few did. I later learned that Mom told them Dad thought she was having an affair, and that he was punishing her by taking away her necessities. She asked if they could store her food in their cupboards and freezer. She returned home with an empty wagon, and I hid in the bathroom, mortified. Had she no shame? I heard her on the phone. "You know what I'm thinkin'? I should bring my silver tea set over there. His golf clubs, too. I'm gonna have to sell this stuff if I wanna eat."

One afternoon, she dug into the dark part of the closet where Dad kept his porn collection. She tossed dozens of VHS tapes into the wagon.

"Mom," I said.

"I don't wanna hear it, C.C. These things aren't cheap. They're expensive to buy. I'm gonna hock 'em. I'm gonna get somethin' out of 'em. For once."

Off she went, pulling the wagon, and I telepathically begged God to combust me into flames. Looking panicked, helpless, she returned, mascara running, porn tapes still in the wagon. She hung on the side of the refrigerator a list of phone numbers. Safe houses for her to go to.

The salesmen's sons were on the baseball team, so the baseball team was the first to find out. Passing them in the hall on my way to first period, I felt their weird smirks in my stomach. After that, every class I entered, conversation stopped or shifted. I witnessed the shocked and horrified expressions on people's faces when they looked at me, but something in my psychological makeup didn't allow me to experience the full onslaught of shame. I went deep inside myself. I felt my body harden into something bulletproof. Mindful of my posture, I walked to my desk as quickly as possible, sat down, and directed every ounce of my attention to the inside of my backpack. Ferociously digging through it, I pretended to search for something I had lost and desperately needed.

As if Mom's having sex with Jay wasn't sensational enough, wilder stories were invented. I had had a threesome with my mom and Jay. Mom was pregnant with Jay's baby. My popularity rank fell. But it was sort of imperceptible. Or only vaguely perceptible. And this caused havoc. Girls from the basketball team who, for years, were used to my being above them in the social hierarchy suddenly didn't know how to react or behave in my company. We'd be on the court, I would give them direction or encouragement, and they'd just look at me with big eyes—a mixture of fear, disbelief, confusion—as if they were trying and failing to compute *my* conflict. My most popular friends were the only ones who felt comfortable talking about it. They weren't shocked about what had happened; they were shocked that I was still attending school. If their moms had had sex with their boyfriends, they said, they would have run away, dropped out, done whatever they wanted. "Utmost freedom," my friend Jessie called it: "You have utmost freedom."

I experienced how it felt to be looked down on, to have

people feel bad for me. "You know you can stay with us for a few nights," random parents said. "You can come for dinner anytime you want." I smiled and thanked them, but there was no way I was going to anybody's house, for anything. One of the dads from the basketball team drove me home from some event. "I heard about your mother," he said. It was the first time someone, an adult, had mentioned it out loud. Inside, I melted in humiliation, but I tried to act like it was no big deal. "I think it happens a lot," I said.

"Not in my circle," he said.

We were in his Land Rover Discovery II. It had a large, tinted sunroof. The filtered light spilled over us as we sat in the gorgeous camel-colored leather seats. How I felt in that moment is why I've never spoken of what happened, until now. It gives people the wrong impression of my upbringing. People assume I grew up white trash. But it wasn't like that. We were a normal middle-class American family. It was a treat for us to go out for seafood. We played sports in the driveway. Whatever emotions I felt for my family I thought of as love.

Mom called her sisters. She left messages. "It's Mary Kay. I need help. Somebody's fillin' Calvis's head full of bullshit. Sayin' that I had an affair. He's taken my car. He's taken the credit cards. There's nothin' to eat in this house. Please. Call me."

Finally, the phone rang. Aunt Sissy told Mom the truth: Dad had been in touch. He'd told them everything. He had tapped the phone lines. There were tapes. Video footage, too. The last one was a lie, but Mom's sisters didn't know that, and now Mom didn't, either.

"Your father has turned everyone against me," she said,

eyes swollen from crying. "He's ruined me. You know what those little towns are like. You know what my sisters are like. I have no place now. I have nothing."

One late afternoon, the doorbell rang—a blip in the universe; it made me panic. Who would willingly come to *us*? Someone not smart. Or someone unaware or unafraid. Mom seemed uneasy about it, too. She slipped into the dining room, out of sight, away from any windows. Through the front door's glass panel, I saw tall bodies, distorted heads. I opened the door.

It was a bunch of guys from my school. Pete Davies, Scott Dickens, Chris Alvarez, Jordy Kleen, the Ruggerelo brothers. Their lower lips bulged with dip, and I could smell it. A sickening mix of mint Tic Tacs and barbecue.

"Hi," I said, nervously. A few more heads peeked out from behind the pillar.

These guys weren't my friends. None of them had been to my house before. Pete Davies did the talking: "Your dad comin' home? You think he'd be mad if we came in?" He spit.

I wanted to laugh it off, tell them they were acting weird and they should leave. I wanted to do it in a charming, unthreatening way. But I could tell by their shared glances that they knew I was scared, and I could tell that they liked it. I shut the door and locked it.

Through the glass, I watched them pick up their bikes and walk them down the driveway. Mom joined me in the hallway. She watched them, too. "What the hell was that about?" she said.

Dad sent me to Publix for kielbasa. I stole them and kept the money. Walking fast down the frozen-food aisle, package tucked into my waistband, I felt their coldness against my skin. From the corner of my eye, I saw movement. A silver glimmer of shopping cart. A flash of milky white skin.

"C.C.?"

It was Jay's mom.

"Hi," I said.

She looked into my eyes. Tilted her head. "Everything okay?" she said.

"Yeah. Why?" I said. It didn't seem like she knew. Or did she?

"I was sorry to hear about you and Jay," she said.

What did she hear?

"I liked the two of you together. I really did. Have you spoken with him? He doesn't tell me anything."

I shook my head.

"He signed up for the Marines. Six years' active duty. Two in reserve." She let out a sigh.

I think I'd thought someone would help Jay. In my mind, he had told his mom, and I was thinking his mom might press charges. Or his guidance counselor would call my guidance counselor, something like that. But nobody helped him. Not his parents, not mine, not me. I think it's because we saw him as someone who didn't need protection or help. He was poor. He had muscles.

His mom pulled me in for a hug. I felt her softness, and the cold kielbasa slipping down my leg.

The seniors marched the halls of Loxahatchee High one last time. Girls in Daisy Dukes rode on their boyfriends' backs. Pigs greased with K-Y Jelly ran through the halls. People tried and failed to catch them. The Offspring blared in the parking lot. Everyone piled into their decorated pickup trucks and did shots and bong hits all the way down Seminole Pratt Road. Sitting in traffic alone, I turned up my radio and pretended to enjoy the song.

The second I stepped inside, the house felt strange to me. It was still. The windows shut, the TV off—and that TV was never off. The only sound was a distant neighbor mowing the lawn. I checked the garage to see if the 'Vette was in there. It wasn't. The Styrofoam float drifted around the pool. I crept down the hallway.

My bedroom looked the same as I'd left it. Lorraine's room was neat and spare, as it always was.

In my parents' room, the bed was made; the sheets were pulled up over the flat white pillows. I was surprised: I hadn't realized Mom was still making Dad's bed. I pulled up the bed skirt. What I was looking for, I had no idea. Snickers's green eyes reflected. His ears were tucked straight back.

The bathroom was dark, but I didn't turn on the light. I opened Mom's makeup drawer and pulled out a lipstick, a shiny cranberry color. I brought it to my lips and looked in the mirror. I saw her in the reflection.

She was sitting on the toilet. Her elbows were on her knees. Her hands gripped something long and black. A snake, I thought. She was going to the bathroom, it came up out of the drain, and she was strangling it, keeping it from slithering out of the bowl. That's exactly what it looked like. I took a step closer to her. It wasn't a snake. It was a shotgun. She was holding it upright, muzzle pressed against her forehead. I backed out of the bathroom.

I backed out of their bedroom. I got to the hallway, turned, and ran. Never before had that hallway seemed so long. I wondered if Mom was following behind, turning the gun on me. I covered my head to protect myself.

I locked my bedroom door. I lay down on my side, plugged my ears tight, and focused on my fishbowl. If the water jumped, that meant the gun had gone off. At least that's what I told myself.

My room got darker. I stayed like that, on my side, ears plugged, staring at the fishbowl, until headlights swept my face. Dad was home. I ran to the front door.

"Pumpkin!" He flipped on the lights.

"Mom's in the bathroom. She has a gun. I think she's gonna kill herself."

He opened the cupboard, grabbed the potato chips. "What does she have, the twenty-two or the twenty?"

"I don't know!"

"Is it long or short?"

"Long."

"The shotgun. It's got a clip on it. She'll never figure it out."

He sat on the couch and turned on the TV.

———— **16.** ————

SUMMER BROUGHT HURRICANE SEASON: SUBTROPI-
CAL depressions, storm-force winds. Dark-green waves
bombed beaches on every channel. Surfers in fluorescent rash guards ran toward them. Meteorologists spoke into
microphones covered in condoms to keep them dry. "What *is*
landfall?" they asked. "What are you *truly* facing when
you're in the eye of the storm? Tonight at seven." Drenched,
Loxahatchee fogged and steamed.

Mom rarely left my room, and when she did, she brought
the shotgun. She'd hold it with both hands, muzzle up, and
set it on the kitchen counter to get a glass of water, or atop the
dryer to do a load of whites. Dad thought it was funny. She'd
turn the corner, and he'd chuckle and say, "Here comes Elmer
Fudd." I was terrified the thing would go off—on purpose or

accidentally. Every time the ice maker rattled, I jumped. I begged her to give me the gun. She shook her head. "I want to kill your father. I just don't have the nerve. Yet."

She destroyed his belongings. Yellow sunlight shot through the drizzle, and Dad's pants, socks, and swimming trunks hung from wet trees. Using the end of the pool skimmer, he lifted a pair of Fruit of the Looms that were snagged on bark. Mosquitoes buzzed around our heads.

"You're doin' it," he said.

"No, I'm not."

"Get your shoes on. We're goin' to the courthouse."

"I'm not going."

"There's people who can help her, Pumpkin."

In Florida, if a close friend or family member can convince a judge that a loved one is a danger to herself or others, that person is taken to a psych ward for an evaluation. This involuntary psychiatric hold is called the Baker Act, and it's sneaky: everyone's in on it except for the one being committed. Mr. Gruber, our athletic director, was Baker Acted. He was a goofy, talkative guy. Slowly, we started noticing that he wasn't showing up to any of the sports events. Then, one day, there was Mr. Gruber, working the checkout at Publix, subdued, and with a beard. Kit LaRocca was also Baker Acted. She got a crush on the math teacher, Ms. McCormick, and, next thing you knew, Kit was gone. Months later, she returned, pink highlights washed out, nose ring removed, Hot Topic wardrobe replaced with Ann Taylor.

If Dad had Mom Baker Acted, she'd be sent to the 45th Street Mental Health Center. It was in a rough part of town. Mentally ill drug addicts—that's who she'd be watching *Good Morning America* with.

Mom would not be able to endure locked rooms and strip searches, and Dad knew it. But without my assistance, he was helpless. He couldn't Baker Act Mom on his own; he said the court required sworn testimonies from two people.

"You're doin' it," Dad said, this time raising his voice. "Your mother is not in her right mind."

"Either are you!"

Yes, Mom seemed crazy. I was afraid of her and for her. I was also afraid for my father, which was confusing for me because, in my mind, his revenge and control tactics had driven Mom to this point. He was the one that posed the biggest threat to our household—not the gun. And if he kept pushing, Mom would kill herself, or us, or everybody. So, to me, Mom didn't need a mental institution; she needed the means to get away from Dad. A one-bedroom apartment she could afford and a thousand dollars a month in alimony: *that* would put an end to her suffering.

"I've given you everything," Dad said. "Easy come, easy go. Right, kid?" He let out a little laugh, the same one he used when fighting with Mom. The one that said: *What a taker.*

Later, in the kitchen, he called the Baker Act hotline. Waiting to get through to a counselor, he put the phone on speaker and made himself a Jack and Coke. "Please stay on the line. You have reached Crisis Services of the Palm Beaches. If someone you love is out of control . . ."

I was taking a side, and it wasn't his; I knew that's why he was mad at me. But I suddenly felt conflicted about *not* doing it. Maybe I was wrong. Maybe Mom really did need doctors.

"Dad, can we just talk about this?"

"Forget it."

"No. I feel bad."

"I said forget it. Sorry I even asked. I'll take care of it."

Wanting to connect with him, I poured myself a Jack and Coke, too.

Dad called Mom's friends. One by one, voice steady, low, peppered with the slightest hint of desperation, he gave his pitch. "I'm worried to death about Mary Kay. I have guns missin'. I'm sure you heard about her and C.C.'s boyfriend. It's a sick type of thing. Very, very sick. Not to put Mary Kay down. This is not why I'm callin' you. She's . . . I'm losing her. She's gonna kill herself. None of us will ever see her again. I'm probably going about this totally the wrong way, but I don't know where else to turn. I need someone to help me get my wife psychiatric help. If I could just sit down with you girls . . ."

They said, "Of course." They'd help in any way they could. Dad reserved a conference room at the Howard Johnson on Okeechobee Boulevard.

On the morning of the "intervention," as he called it, Dad got dressed up—pressed pants, crisp white polo. I jumped into the pool and swam. I didn't know if he was expecting me to come with him or not, and I didn't know what I was going to say if he asked me to. When it came to strategizing against my father, I found it impossible to have any kind of plan. He was a master manipulator. There was no outsmarting him, exposing him, reasoning with him. There wasn't any protecting myself from him. All I could do was observe.

Through the sliding glass doors, I watched him cut a fresh lime, then pour a gin and tonic into a thirty-two-ounce Styrofoam cup. He checked his watch against the microwave clock and slipped out the laundry-room door.

That evening, he called. "You got somewhere to go? I'd get outta there if I were you."

A part of me thought Dad was bluffing. It felt like an experiment—a way for him to see how I behaved under pressure. But what would bluffing get him at this point? Guidance, for his next move, I thought. A bigger part of me felt that Dad's intervention had worked. He'd talked one of Mom's friends into going with him to the courthouse. Now people were coming to take Mom away. I sneaked a beer—the only thing in the fridge—and sat on the couch with MTV on mute so I'd be sure to hear the sirens. An ambulance, a gurney, Mom strapped to it: that's what I imagined was about to happen.

In the evening, I kept checking on Mom. I listened at the door, considered knocking, and then went back to the couch. When nerves overtook me, I went out onto the porch and practiced my spider-dribbling drills. At some point, Mom went to bed. Under my bedroom door, I saw only a strip of black.

Throughout the night, I woke up in fits. I believed I was being triggered by intuition—*They're preparing the ambulance. The ambulance left the hospital. The ambulance is turning the corner.* It was half past midnight. It was a quarter to three. At five, I heard men laughing. I jumped from the couch and looked out the window. Construction workers walked to their work site. Panic kicked in.

I tried the door. It was unlocked. My room felt foreign. It smelled like depression. The blue haze of dawn seeped through the blinds.

"Mom," I whispered.

She didn't move. The shotgun lay alongside her. Fearing it would go off, I sat on the bed as lightly as I could.

"Mom," I whispered louder. "Do you wanna get breakfast?"

"I'm not goin' to breakfast."

"I think we should go. Come get breakfast with me. Let's go to Denny's," I said.

"Oh no. I ain't goin' there. That place is shitty."

"Get dressed. Sit up." To get her going, I gave her shoulder a little nudge.

"Don't you be pushin' me," she said. She smiled. She thought I was being nice, like I was trying to be her daughter again. I felt like I was tricking a child.

The doorbell rang.

I thought I was going to have a heart attack. Mom shot up and looked at the clock. "Who the hell is this now?" she said.

What was happening was on the tip of my tongue. *Say it.* But I feared her reaction would be irrational. If I told her to hide in the closet, she wouldn't just hide in the closet. She would shoot herself.

She peeked out through the blinds. "Cops." She threw on a robe. "How much you wanna bet your father's in the slammer?" She walked down the hallway. I pulled the sheet over the gun, picked up Snickers, and listened. I heard the crackle of walkie-talkies.

"Mrs. Borkoski? Sergeant Fulton. This is Sergeant Maxwell. You have time for a few questions?"

"Questions about what?"

"Are you on any medication?"

"I don't take medication."

"Any weapons in the house?"

"Weapons?"

"Guns?"

"There was one. I don't know if it's here now or not. You'd

have to talk to my daughter about that. She's always hidin'
it. . . . C.C.!" Mom yelled. "Cops are here. They wanna talk
to you!"

Oh no.

"I'm here to talk to you, Mrs. Borkoski."

They must've noticed something in Mom's expression, because, next thing I knew, they were explaining that they were
gonna have to put her in handcuffs.

I heard the slap of Mom's bare feet running on the tile. I
heard grabbing, grunting. I walked out of the hallway and
saw the cops low to the ground. Mom was on her stomach.
Her face was twisted, and it looked like she was howling, but
no sound was coming out. Then came a wail.

Snickers jerked, scratched, and tried to get out of my arms.
I held him tighter. The cops grabbed Mom's wrists and pulled
her to her feet. They spun her around and I was caught off
guard by how rough they were. She yelled at me to call 911.
"And tell them what?" I said.

"This!" Mom yelled. "This!"

I looked at the cops. Their tight haircuts made me feel that
if I went for the phone they would shoot me. I asked them for
permission. "Am I allowed to pick up the phone?" I said.
They manhandled Mom out the front door.

Snickers still in my arms, I followed them outside. There
was a fire truck, an ambulance, several cop cars, and in the
middle of it all stood Dad.

"You got your little fuckin' tape recorder on, Calvis?"
Mom yelled.

"What tape recorder are you talking about?" Dad said.

To avoid getting too close to her, he walked up the side of

the grass, taking big steps over the fire-ant piles. He stood so close to me I could feel his arm hair.

"Get this on tape, Cal: You're a lowlife bastard. You been screwin' around on me since the first year we were married. You don't love me. You never did."

The cop put his hand atop Mom's head. He tried to push her into the back seat of the cruiser. She didn't budge.

"You sit back and take it from anybody who'll give it to ya. I'm takin' you for every goddamn thing you got, you lousy fuckin' son of a bitch."

"There ain't nothin' left, Mary Kay. We're broke."

"How the hell you buyin' your hooker ribs for dinner, then? I saw the receipt in the garbage. Two full racks."

"We didn't go to dinner."

The cop struggled to pick Mom up.

"You jealous, Mary Kay?"

"I'm not jealous. You're sick."

"I'm sick? Where you think you're off to in that cruiser, hon?"

Mom looked at me. I'd never seen her so furious. "One day you're gonna need your mother," she said. The power with which those words hit the air made them feel like a curse.

It took two cops to lift Mom off her feet and slide her sideways into the back seat, like a surfboard. They sped out the driveway, lights flashing. Neighbors gathered on the sidewalk, their front porches, and the road. They didn't even pretend to be out there to get their newspapers. They just stared.

I loosened my grip on Snickers. My chest and neck were covered in puffy pink scratches. Dad looked at me with the saddest eyes.

"What do you think, Pumpkin? Did I take it too far?"

— 17. —

THERE'S NO SUCH THING AS "the wild." It's curated, just like a museum. Drones patrol the oceans and land. They identify the whistle of birds colliding with power lines. They spot the tentacles of endangered creatures wrapped around coral, a tail partially hidden in a cave. They determine the best locations for deploying seed pods and shoot them into the ground. Their pneumatic arms inject poison into anything they deem to be destructive. The first drone invented to pursue conservation goals was named Bev. Twenty seconds into flight, she concluded that the only way to stop light pollution was to eliminate humans. She misidentified her local Walmart as a group of poachers.

From the drone's clouds, millions of photos are sent to scientists. They use them for all kinds of things, but mostly to keep an eye on apex predators. This is how they know the moment a baby orca is born, and the exact location of every Bengal tiger.

Nobody knows what to do with apex predators. In every way, they have it the worst. The habitat they need, we want for all our stupid shit, and we won't give them an inch. They belong on this earth just like everyone else, but they scare us and make our lives uneasy. Take gray wolves—the most polarizing animal out there. They were federally exterminated. Decades later, they received protection, were bred in captivity, and were re-released into the wild. Once again, they're traveling in packs, walking down the center of dirt roads, leaving behind bloated cow carcasses, costing ranchers thousands of dollars. And, once again, lawmakers are calling to have them killed. They have a saying: "If you like wolves, it's because you live in a place that doesn't have them."

So where are they supposed to go? What are we supposed to do? Conservation groups believe they have the answer. Working with the ranchers, they've started putting people (college interns) in the fields with the cattle. Their job is to stand there and oversee them, like modern-day shepherds.

Shortly after my divorce, I was Airbnb'ing a place in New Haven when Lorraine began preparing for her release from prison, just outside Chillicothe, Ohio. During her seven-year sentence (repeated drug offenses, aggravated robbery), she lost custody of Desiree. She also overdosed on heroin and fentanyl. She didn't die, but she wasn't okay, either. Her brain was on cognitive delay. It took her about twenty seconds to comprehend an elementary conversation. Her parole officer recommended that I put her in a state nursing home. I researched a few near New Haven. I stopped by one to take a look. Old people moaned. Many of them were bed-bound. Lorraine was thirty-two. She still listened to heavy metal. I told her parole officer that the environment seemed too slow for her.

"That's the point," he said.

He talked me through the immediate challenges she'd encounter moving from confinement to freedom. She needed civilian clothes, a means to get to the residence into which she was to be released, and food to sustain her as she navigated her first few hours on the outside. She also required "gate money"—some minimal amount of cash on hand to fulfill these immediate needs. He recommended $109. Lorraine didn't have any of these things.

There were no resources in Adena, or any of the surrounding small towns. No clinics, therapists, shelters, public transportation. Nothing. So Lorraine would never be able to follow up on her release plan. If she went to a bigger city—say, Columbus—the kind of problem she had (neurological damage) would prevent her from being able to read bus routes and seek out services.

Lorraine had nothing to return to, no home, car, job, money, child. I, alone, was her support system. In the days leading up to her release date, I gave my notice at Ardsley.

I-70 rushed toward me in the headlights, and I began to see all the familiar exit signs. Ohio Welcome Center; OH-331, Flushing; US-40, National Road. I experienced a very sudden and unexpected homesickness. I put on my blinker.

Along the roller-coaster hills, industrial well sites glowed like UFOs in the night. Trailers were set up with flags and signs: twenty-four-hour gas permits. Drills cranked and groaned as they fracked the land. Sitting in truck traffic, I rolled up my window to blunt the noise, but it still sounded like a helicopter was hovering over me.

At the base of Adena's welcome sign, atop fresh mulch and blooming marigolds, the Virgin Mary prayed. Stigmata stains gone, she was bright white. She'd been pressure-washed.

Among the exposed pipelines, compressors, and high-decibel hums, food wagons sold chili and hats made from groundhog pelts—perfect for the out-of-town drillers who were unprepared for the cold.

A new Dodge Ram was parked in front of Aunt Sissy's house. I knocked on the door.

"C.C.! What are you doin' here? I thought you were the Jehovah Witness."

Aunt Cookie and Aunt Connie were there, too. They hugged me, and I smelled their powdery makeup. I noticed they were wearing earplugs. They took a break from the card game, cut salami and cheese, and got right down to gossip. Talking above one another, they overflowed with stories about the fracking boom. They all had pipelines on their properties; the government paid them seven thousand dollars per acre. Aunt Cookie and Aunt Connie had eight acres. Aunt Sissy had twenty-five. Her house had been completely remodeled. She showed me the new, long deck, and the stainless-steel grill. Room to room, she pointed out the refurbished fireplace, the hardwood floors. Mirror holders and screws poked out of the bare walls. Because of vibrations from the drilling, nothing could be hung on them. They were cracked. The ceiling was too.

Their kids had jobs—good ones—as surveyors and waste haulers. A few of them had been trained to work on the rigs. They talked about an upcoming cruise they were taking to the Bahamas. "It's about time I see the world," Aunt Connie said. She jabbed her Kool into the ashtray.

They referred to my mother as "the big champion of romance," and asked if I was going to see her. I didn't give them an answer, and they didn't press it. Aunt Sissy heated me up meatloaf and boiled me tap water for the road.

Last I heard, Mom was working at the JCPenney at the Fort Steuben Mall. The parking lot was filled with F-150s and Ram 1500s, their plates from Louisiana and Texas. I had to circle it twenty times before I found a parking space. I walked from department to department. I spotted Mom in Men's.

It was the first time I'd seen her since that morning in the driveway, thirteen years ago. She had on glasses and a pink sweatshirt with a huge face of a tabby cat, its whiskers sparkling. She had rings on every finger, even her thumb. There was a long line leading to her register. Everyone in it was wearing a cowboy hat. I joined them. Each time she said "Next," my heart beat faster.

"Next!"

I walked up to the counter. "Find everything okay?" she said. Only when I smiled did she recognize me. "Oh my God," she gasped. We didn't hug. She just kept saying "Oh my God" and I kept smiling. When the customers behind me grew impatient, I stood to the side. "That's my daughter," Mom said, checking them out. At close, she counted her register. I could tell she was nervous, too: she kept losing track of her count.

I don't know how long my mother stayed at the mental hospital. Three days? Three months? Due to confidentiality laws, the nurses would never confirm whether she was even there. "It's up to the patient to decide who they want to talk to," they said. Mom never returned my calls.

At some point, my aunts paid for Mom's plane ticket, and she moved back to Adena. Aunt Vi let her move in. She paid her ninety dollars a week to care for her daughter, who had breast cancer. It was cheaper than paying for a nurse.

My cousin refused chemotherapy and went the alternative route: shark cartilage, grapefruit. Day and night, Mom stayed by her side, making her soup, reading her passages from *The Celestine Prophecy*. My cousin's fiancé drove them as far as Pittsburgh for doctors' appointments. The three of them spent a lot of time together in doctors' offices and waiting rooms. Mom saw in the fiancé someone who gave everything he had, did everything he could, for a woman he loved. Wanting that for herself, she seduced him.

This time, Mom didn't treat it like a secret. She had found true love. She and the fiancé came out as a couple. He was twenty-two years younger than her. My aunts called me in utter disbelief. "Your mother keeps sayin' it's not a big deal, that lots of people meet at funerals. It's like she doesn't even realize that her niece is still alive!"

"I understand, completely," I said.

Mom clocked out. Security walked us through the dark mall. Workers slid the security gates over Spencer Gifts, Orange Julius, a truck-driving school, a funeral parlor.

"How's married life, kid?" Mom said.

I forgot that she knew I had gotten married. Alex was already dating someone.

"It's good. Great," I said.

We hit the parking lot. "Don't laugh," she said. "I'm drivin' a car that has two hundred thousand miles on it."

"Why would I laugh?" I said.

Over the next few days, I stayed with her. Mom's sisters had chased her out of Adena. And because of the fracking boom, rents had more than doubled. Mom lived in a trailer on the outskirts of Steubenville, a short walk to the fracking waste well. It looked like an enormous, decrepit swimming pool, covered by a tarp. There weren't any NO TRESPASSING signs. Nothing that said anything about chemicals. There was just a big guy in a brown security-guard outfit sitting in a camp chair. And up the hill, a bull for sale. He'd gone sterile from drinking frack water.

There was so much I'd forgotten about living in a single-wide. The thinness of the walls; how cold the rooms were in the mornings. Lying in bed, listening to Mom make coffee, I could see my breath. Back when we owned the dealership, Dad was so smart he included our singlewide as part of the floor plan. Like it was just another car we could resell. Of course, we had no intention of reselling it. It was our home, just twenty-two steps from Parts. The bedroom I shared with Lorraine looked over the two-acre lot and the rows of shiny cars with vinyl tops. Before bed, we'd gaze out the window. Quartz glittered like tiny stars in the asphalt, and we'd take turns wishing for our favorite car. The one we hoped to buy below invoice in our imaginary future.

There was so much I had forgotten about my mother, too. How excited she got over small things, like broccoli-and-cheese soup, and spotting trouble in her favorite soaps

("Tommy and Marie sure are sittin' close at that dinner table"). She showed me the deals she scored at T.J. Maxx. Modeling her latest purchase in the living room, turning this way and that, she smoothed the fur collar. "Honestly, it's one of the few impractical things I've done in my life, is buy a white coat to shovel snow in, in all this dirt and grime."

I learned new things about my mother, as well. Most of her friends were very young—younger than Lorraine and me. She went to happy hours with them after work and they drank mudslides. Every time we got into the car, she played Taylor Swift.

Our dynamic was so ingrained that there was no deleting it: Mom talked; I listened. The difference was that her problems were more interesting. She spoke of issues with her co-workers and managers, and the labor shortage: nobody could pass a drug test. Wanting to get back in touch with God, she was checking out different churches. There was one she liked. It was in a basement. There were rappers there, and footlongs from Subway. Mom listened to rap music, ate the subs, and talked about redemption. "They invited me back! I said, 'Why not?'"

One night, she showed me her Facebook page. As she scrolled past selfie after selfie, it struck me how good she was at taking them. She knew her angles, and the best spots in her trailer for natural lighting. Taken in the bedroom, the living room, the bathroom, she looked up at the camera. Fresh makeup, hand touching her face—rings shimmering—she smiled.

Here was a woman in her fifties who had done unspeakable things to immediate family members. She had no contact whatsoever with either of her children. Her granddaughter was a teenager and she had yet to meet her. So much rupture, so much severing, yet she showed not an iota of pain, shame, or self-consciousness. She looked beautiful. And proud.

Seeing her in her natural habitat, I realized how far she had come. No alimony, no work experience, a high-school diploma from thirty-five years ago, and she was making her own way in the world. I respected that.

On my last morning in town, Mom insisted on taking me to see the new rail trail. A present to the local community from the Oil & Gas company, it was a two-mile-long paved path through the old train tunnel. Inside, it was dark, cold, and moist. Mom and I stayed in there for a long time, watching the water stream down the tunnel walls.

At the end of the path was an arbor with a gazebo. I joined the very long line for the single porta-potty. When I returned, I spotted Mom in the gazebo, talking to a guy. Her face was animated. She was laughing, smiling. I joined them, and she wrapped up the conversation. "I'm glad I ran into you, Bob. I really like talkin' to you. We should meet here sometime, walk the tunnel together."

"Oh no, Mary Kay," he said. He softened the blow with a chuckle. "My wife wouldn't like that very much. You've got a reputation. You're a bad girl."

Mom's face dropped. Mine must've, too. I couldn't believe that this man, *Bob,* with his beer belly and John Deere baseball cap, had said what he just said. Part of my shock came from the realization that a stranger knew this about her. For some reason, I'd been under the impression that only family knew the things she had done. The other part of my shock came from how separate I felt from her at this moment. I didn't feel that familiar, all-consuming family shame. It just felt like I was watching someone get called out. I felt embarrassed for her, but I, personally, didn't feel embarrassed.

I felt Bob glance at me. Even though I didn't look at him, I felt his confusion. It's like he didn't understand why the mood had so drastically changed. I don't think he knew I was Mom's daughter. I think he thought I was one of her happy-hour buddies.

"What the hell was that man talkin' about?" Mom said, waiting to make a left onto Route 9.

"Put your blinker on, Mom."

"*Reputation. Bad girl.* I am a fifty-three-year-old woman."

"After this car."

"His wife wouldn't like that. Gimme a break. That man's wife hasn't slept with him in twenty-five years."

The back road ambled alongside a winding creek. Barbed-wire fencing surrounded a rotting black barn with the words CHEW MAIL POUCH TOBACCO painted white across its side. I recognized the view. The rolling hills, the lay of the asphalt, the tall white lights. It was our old car lot. All hundred acres of it. *I would have been a rich man,* Henry Flagler once said, *if it hadn't been for Florida.*

An oil rig rose from the ground, and its slender tower threw a shadow over the fracking engines, multiple oil wells, and gravel pit. A fleet of trucks piped out the oil and gas.

The drill broke the bedrock. For an instant, a patch of asphalt caught fire. Coal combusting flammable gases, a gasoline rainbow reaching the sky.

The sun wasn't up and it was thirty degrees. Lorraine stood at the gate in orange prison scrubs, and what looked to be my grandpa's coal-mining boots. I pulled up beside her and rolled down the window. Mist felt soft on my face.

"It's good to see you," I said.

"You too, dude."

I thought she'd be in a rush to get out of this place, but she lingered, taking long drags from her cigarette, looking at me with wide eyes.

No guardrails. No traffic. No leaves on the trees. In a nearby park of ground cement and glass, she changed into the clothes I'd brought her. "You're my numero uno," she said, feeling the pockets on the jeans, and again when sliding on her new shoes. We sat in the car with the windows down. In the visor mirror, she tousled her bangs.

"If you don't let me live with you, I'm gonna have to move into a homeless shelter. I'm gonna get lice and nobody'll ever wanna marry me." She flipped up the visor. "I'd be better off hitchhiking to Florida. Maybe Ted Bundy'll pick me up and kill me, and then I'll be dead and everybody'll be happy."

"Ted Bundy's dead," I said. I brought my coffee to my lips, then started to laugh at the outrageousness of the conversation. Lorraine started to laugh, too.

"No, he's not, dude," she said, smiling.

"Yes, he is! He got the electric chair."

"So what am I gonna do?"

"I found a place for you. It's all set up."

A light, hypnotic riff came from the radio. Lorraine turned it up. Sharing a sleeve of Chips Ahoy!, we enjoyed the Led Zeppelin rock block.

I landed a job at the Florida Zoo. As director of storytelling, sales, and marketing, I developed humanizing narratives that boosted attendance and revenue. I wrote *everything:* the director's speeches, keeper talks, signage, the trends report, animal obituaries, pieces of advancement collateral to present to potential donors illustrating new exhibit concepts. I even had to make our annual revenue report narratively compelling.

Compared with Ardsley, my higher-ups were much less uptight, even permissive. We didn't have to wear uniforms. Visible tattoos didn't raise any eyebrows, and face piercings were allowed without comment. The "campus," as the zoo was called, consisted of long vistas and large habitats with a naturalistic feel. Log and rock features gave off heat when it dipped below seventy. The steamy, woodsy vibe gave the impression that you were really one with the animals. A network of overhead "sky trails" suspended by wires allowed them to traverse above the grounds. So guests had to watch not only around them for animals, but also overhead. Some guests weren't aware that the trails existed. They'd be walking around, lost in thought, enjoying themselves, when, suddenly, they'd look up and see a lioness intently watching them. They'd let out high-pitched screams, and then compose themselves. "Dear God. I thought it got out of its cage." One older man had a heart attack. I watched the animals watch the paramedics give him CPR.

At my first weekly meeting, I pitched my idea for the Homeless Animal Shelter exhibit. I don't think the zoo president, Mr. Chase, even looked up from the box of Dunkin' Donuts. "Go for it," he said. Sitting with the exhibit curator, brainstorming form and function, I got a little concerned about the number of animal hammocks tied between trees.

"Do you think it's okay that the only thing the homeless animals are doing is . . . loafing?" I said.

"Good point. Might irritate the guests." He thought for a moment. "Let's give 'em a pool."

It felt great to be appreciated at my job. I was even allowed to develop a newsletter. *10-100*—walkie-talkie code for animal escape—laid bare the everyday goings-on inside the zoo: the disposal of rhino organs following a necropsy, the anteater's erectile dysfunction stemming from his diabetes, and his mate's subsequent behavior (she followed around the Patagonian cavy named Uncle Jimmy and slept beside him every night). I even profiled the zoo's dentist as he went through a high-profile divorce with Ji, the top plastic surgeon in town. These stories were built on a sense of place, and a feel for the local. I got us sponsorships. Some of the stories from *10-100* got mentioned on morning radio shows. It unlocked a treasure trove of donor contributions and loyalty from repeat visitors. Attendance skyrocketed. After just eight months, I got a raise.

There was only one problem.

The zoo's biggest donor, Renee Cutter, didn't believe in climate change. She forbade the use of the phrases "global warming," "climate change," and "climate collapse" in any of the zoo documents. She said this, explicitly; Mr. Chase even had to sign a contract agreeing to it. He put together a "verbiage guide" of all the contentious words I had to stay away from. Renee Cutter gave us millions (and millions) of dollars to help the most mangled, malnourished of animals. No matter how destroyed a bat's face was from white-nose syndrome, she never turned any of them away. She helped raise five million dollars for our hospital—the Renee Cutter Care Compound and Wildlife Rehab—which won every award imaginable for veterinary technologies. Two Tesla MRI scanners for precise medical diagnosis in horses, isolation stalls providing the highest level of biosecurity to treat animals with infectious disease, inpatient hospital services, including advanced small-species dental diagnostics and surgery (ferret, root canal). I had no choice but to play Renee Cutter's game. I just didn't know how. Coming up with our new and improved mission statement was the mindfuck of the century.

"If we don't exist for conservation reasons, why do we exist?" I said.

"Entertainment," my co-worker said.

"Too outdated," I said.

"Maybe . . . to inspire people?" the CFO said.

"How so?" I said.

"To enjoy nature?" she said.

"No, no," I said. "No."

"By *not* trying to convert every guest into a world-changing activist on a wild mission to straighten out anyone they perceive as bad guys," Mr. Chase said.

"I like that. But if that's what we *don't* do, what do we do?" I said.

"You're good with words," Mr. Chase said. "You'll think of something."

18.

 IN THE HEAT AND RAIN, our yard grew wild. Vines and branches hung like nets from the trees. Every day, there were more armadillo holes. Dad didn't even try to keep up with the grass.

I could no longer enjoy sips of Beefeater in a Dixie cup while dipping my feet in the pool. The water had turned murky green; the steps were furred with black algae. I found it so upsetting, but Dad wasn't bothered by it at all. Preparing for his afternoon nap, he played George Jones's "He Stopped Loving Her Today" on the stereo and pulled the patio doors wide open, as though the view were still inviting, the water still turquoise and sparkling.

The phone never stopped. Debt collectors called from

eight in the morning until ten at night, Sundays too. I wanted to leave the phone off the hook, but Dad wouldn't let me. "In case my girlfriends need me," he said.

Sometimes, in the middle of the night, after the bars closed, Dad came into my room with spools of lottery tickets. He used a butter knife; I used a quarter. Sheets sticking to my legs, I scratched quick and hard: 2X, 5X, 10X, win up to 35X the amount shown.

"You're goin' too fast, C.C. Double-check those. You're gonna throw away a million bucks."

Outside, I shook the silver scratchings from the comforter. They flew everywhere, like sand from a beach towel.

Sometimes debt collectors came to the door. Dad covered the glass panel with a bedsheet so they couldn't look inside. Snickers kept his distance. "What's a matter, Snickers?" Dad said. "You don't talk to me no more."

Dad tried to get his old job back at Les Russo Ford. Every day, he either called or stopped by. Finally, the GM left a message: "Hey, Cal, listen, we made some moves with Nelson and the other guy we hired. We're gonna ride with them for a little while, see how that goes. If that's productive for me, I'm gonna stay with them. If it's not, I'll—"

Dad pressed "stop."

On his dresser, I came across ripped-out ads for customer-service positions at rental-car agencies. They paid minimum wage. Dad always said he could walk into any dealership in America and they'd hire him on the spot. Every so often, he went on job interviews. An hour later, he returned. "Nobody wants to hire a drunk," he'd say, or "Your old man's a bum." Happy he was talking, I perked up. "You're not a bum, Dad!"

He'd sleep for thirteen hours, blink himself awake, and sit in his recliner in the dark. With the volume on high, he watched and re-watched the movie *48 Hrs.* Every time a car came on-screen, he announced the make and model. Engine specs, too.

"We need groceries," I said.

"Ya got money?" he said. Then he said he didn't need to eat. In this respect, Dad was a goat. He existed on cans of Miller Lite.

I came home with groceries. He rooted through the bags. "No cookies? What, you don't like cookies? No Cokes? What, you don't like Cokes?"

I didn't know how to cook; I didn't know how to use the oven. So for supper I baked pepperoni rolls on the same heating pad Mom used to soothe her menstrual cramps. We ate at the kitchen counter. Dad sat on one end; I sat on the other. We were separated by outstanding bills, hundreds of them, divided into dozens of small stacks. "You make excellent pepperoni rolls," Dad said. "I sure am lucky to have you. I really am." Long after supper was over, Dad stayed at the counter, head in hands. "Resting," he said.

I found a $399 flat-fee lawyer in the Yellow Pages and made an appointment for a free consultation. Dad tried to get out of it at the last minute. I knew he would. "Dad. Come on. I'm getting mad now."

"Oh yeah?" he said, with a chuckle. But he did get ready. In the bathroom, I watched him dot the tiny red veins on the side of his nose with Mom's old cover-up stick. Drinker's skin concealed, he turned his cheek left, right, admiring himself. He put on his swimming trunks, T-shirt, and Ford baseball cap. He insisted on taking the Mustang.

With the windows down, wind screamed through the front seat and thrashed our hair. Pigs and strawberry fields eventually gave way to gas stations and pawnshops. Past the food bank and Mr. Glow Car Wash stood high-rises. For a split second, I saw mansions and the intracoastal blues and greens. Flash—we were in a bad neighborhood. Dad made me park behind a liquor store.

"Don't tell him we have a Corvette; just tell him we have a Chevy."

"Dad. It's a waste of time and money if we're gonna lie to our lawyer."

"Pumpkin, I do not need a lecture on ethics."

Dad grabbed his briefcase. Street dogs ran loose and barked as we walked past parched yards and up the driveway of Willy G. Whitcomb, Bankruptcy & Accidents.

The office was hot and cramped. A sleeping bag and pillow were stuffed into one corner. I squeezed into a chair facing Willy and, behind him, a framed portrait of Andrew Jackson. Dad sat beside me. There was barely enough room for him to open his briefcase. The dogs' howling intensified. Willy stuck a cigarette into his mouth but didn't light it. He took notes, asked questions:

"Mortgages?"

"Two," Dad said. He set letters in front of Willy. "Wells Fargo, about hundred and five. And a HELOC with Nations, about one sixty."

"Credit cards."

" 'Bout one forty."

"Assets: Boats. Cars."

"A Chevy," Dad said.

"Blue Book?"

"Forty thousand," he said.

Willy looked up from his notes. "That must be some kinda Chevy."

Silence. It had gotten Dad this far—why change now?

Willy gave up and gave us the lowdown. If we went bankrupt and kept the house, we could have up to one thousand dollars of assets. If we went bankrupt and didn't keep the house, we could have up to five thousand dollars in assets.

"Either way, you gotta lose the Chevy," Willy said.

"They take anything into consideration? Single fathers? Nutso wives who went through the change? Kids?" Dad said.

I wasn't really a kid. I'd be eighteen in three months.

"Trustees are hard-nosed people," Willy said.

I asked Willy how long Dad and I had before the bank came with the padlocks.

"Couple weeks, couple months. Who knows? But they're comin'," Willy said, and popped his lighter. His cigarette reached for the flame.

The big, low sun ran along the corner of the windshield. I felt shaky. Dad seemed relieved. He talked about having time, but not about what we had time for. I pulled into the 7-Eleven for gas.

"You got money?" he said.

"Do *you*?" I snapped.

He dug into the waterproof pocket of his trunks and tossed into my lap a wadded-up ten-dollar bill.

"Get me a dozen glazed," he said.

"I'm using it for gas," I said and marched into the 7-Eleven. In line to pay the cashier, I could barely contain my anger.

The line shifted, and the Plexiglas display case and the doughnuts inside came into view. Sweets were the only thing Dad enjoyed anymore. His days were so empty. It must be devastating to have your wife cheat on you with a high schooler.

I pumped the gas. Dad bit into a doughnut. "You think your father's a freeloader," he said. It may or may not have been a question. Either way, it was now my turn to be quiet.

I unpeeled the bright-orange foreclosure notice stuck to our front door. Snickers pressed up to my legs. I felt his matted cat dreadlocks against my skin. "Snickers, kitty. The bank's a-comin'. You gotta be ready to go at a moment's notice," Dad said.

He headed straight to the blinking green light of the answering machine and pressed "play." "Let's see which one of my girlfriends called this time." It was back-to-back automated-message robot-voice debt collectors. Not one human.

I woke up early for school, much earlier than usual. It was still dark outside. The front door was standing open. In the driveway, the driver's-side door of the 'Vette was open, too. I shut both doors, thinking Dad had come home drunk and forgotten to close everything on his stumble in.

I went to make coffee. It was already made. I heard something in the laundry room and pushed the door open just a bit. Dad was kneeling in front of the open dryer, like he was praying to it, worry all over his face.

"Do you want oatmeal?" I said.

"There's no way to go bankrupt and keep the house," he said.

"I know."

"If we go bankrupt, we lose everything."

"I know."

"They ain't gettin' the 'Vette."

"Sell it."

"I ain't sellin' it."

"Sign it over to me."

"You got forty thousand dollars?"

"I don't want to buy the 'Vette. Just pretend I gave you cash. Put it in my name."

He pulled beach towels from the dryer. There were only two of them.

"Dad! Why did you do a full load of laundry for two beach towels?!"

"Stop beatin' up your father."

Something in his demeanor made me nervous. He walked to his bedroom, and into the master bath. I followed, fidgeting.

"You're punishing me. My nerves can't take it," he said to the mirror. He combed his hair straight back, then tossed the comb forcefully back into the drawer.

"Dad. Are you gonna kill yourself?"

I hated to ask, but it was the feeling I was getting.

He placed both hands on the counter and dropped his head. He stayed like that for a long time, and I watched, not saying a word. Not even breathing, I don't think. When he finally looked up at me, his face was so red it was purple. His eyes were bloodshot. I had never seen my father cry, so it took me a minute to realize that's what he was doing. In a voice quieter than before, he said: "Everybody's father leaves sometime, kid. None of us stick around forever."

My instinct was to drop to my knees and cling to him, the

way women did to Christ in movies. The only reason I didn't was that I thought it would make him stop crying, and I wanted him to be able to keep showing emotion.

"It's all gone. . . . *Poof!*" he said.

"We're still here. We're not gone."

He inhaled in a weird way. His cheeks got big. Like he was blowing up a beach ball. His exhale was loud. He grabbed the towel off the rack and wiped his face.

"I need your help," he said.

He walked out of the bathroom. I followed him through the living room, the kitchen, and back to the laundry room. I started to get a very bad feeling.

"Where are we going?" I said. He opened the door to the garage.

I stopped. It felt like, if I went into the garage with him, he was going to talk me into helping him commit suicide. Like he was going to pressure me into wrapping something around his neck and giving him a push off the attic ladder.

"Come on," Dad said.

"No."

"I got somethin' to show you."

"You said you needed my help."

"I do."

"I'm not going in there," I said.

Again, he hung his head. But this time, when he lifted it, he was laughing. He laughed so hard he let out a snort.

"What are you doin', C.C.? You're lettin' bugs in! Come on!"

I went mute. My body froze from the inside out.

Dad went into the garage, leaving the door open just a

crack. I stood in the laundry room and listened. I heard metal scraping. I could tell that what he was moving around was heavy. He was breathing hard, grunting.

I smelled gasoline.

"Dad?"

"You ain't gonna help me, then shut the door," he said.

I pushed it open wider. I could now see most of the garage. Dad was squatting in the far corner.

"Dad, come back in the house."

"You see what I'm doin'?" he said. He was out of breath.

It took all the energy I had to take a few steps closer. I saw that he was pouring gas from the red five-gallon can into the lawn mower.

I tried to make sense of what was going on. My thinking was that once he got the lawn mower's motor started, he was going to put a bag over his head, wrap his mouth around the cap of the tank, and start inhaling the gas. Or maybe pouring gas into the lawn mower was his first step to setting the house on fire. Either way, why did he need me? What was my role? He grabbed my hand and pulled me toward him.

"No!" I yelled. It didn't seem like he heard me. Or maybe I hadn't yelled at all. He pushed my fingers around the mower's handle. "Grip it tight," he said. He took my other hand and wrapped it around the pull cord at the rear wheels. "Ready?" he said.

I was close to tears, but it was like I was too scared to cry. The smell of gasoline grew so overpowering, I thought I was going to pass out from the fumes. That's when it occurred to me that maybe that was the point. Maybe he was going to kill both of us.

"Pull it!" he said.

I pulled the cord. It didn't budge. My whole body was shaking. I was too weak, and there was too much resistance.

"You gotta pull it *back*," he said.

"I can't."

"Put force into it, C.C."

"I don't have any!"

"Now you're pissin' me off," he said. His nostrils flared.

I steadied myself and put my entire body into pulling the cord. Again. Then again. Finally, the engine rumbled. Palmetto bugs the size of birds flew up to the ceiling.

"The-e-e-e-re. There you go!" he said. A heartbeat pounded in my head. I waited for a fire to ignite, or for Dad to start killing us. He hit the button on the wall.

The garage door lifted, revealing a warm breeze, the smell of pine, and long, thick, wet grass. I turned my attention back to Dad, to the two deep lines in his forehead, bubbling with sweat. "Now you know how to start a gas mower, you can start any mower out there," he said with a dramatic sweep of his arm. "Can't put a price tag on that."

He walked into the house, and I stood there, gripping the loud, vibrating lawn mower, trying to come down from the violence I had imagined while also trying to understand what had just taken place. Why was it so important that I learn how to start the lawn mower? Was I now supposed to cut the grass? Was he trying to show me a way to make money? He walked out the door with a cup of coffee and two beach towels, and slid into the 'Vette. "See ya, Pumpkin," he said, and backed out the driveway.

At first, when he didn't come home, I thought maybe he was embarrassed about getting emotional and scaring me, so he spent a few nights on the beach to cool down. I remember feeling relieved that he was taking some time for himself. But then nights passed, and he didn't come home for dinner.

I barely slept, and when I did my mind stayed up and worried. Debt collectors' calls were incessant, but I didn't dare take the phone off the hook. What if Dad tried to reach me? For money, I pawned some of his tools. Getting gas at the Shell station, I could've sworn I saw him come out of the men's bathroom. I turned my head back to the pump for a second, and when I looked back, he wasn't there. One morning, I walked into the kitchen, and I *knew* Dad was in the house. I could feel his presence, smell his Old Spice. My body didn't allow my mind the chance to veto the desire to call out to him, "Dad?" Waiting for him to answer, I started to think that maybe he had died and that he was trying to contact me from the afterlife. I got the feeling that maybe he had shot himself in the pool. I grabbed the pole with the skimmer attached, lowered it into the dark-green water, and jabbed it around to see if I'd hit his body.

It's embarrassing to say, but it took me about eight days to understand that my dad had walked out on me. I began experiencing a sensation of feeling absolutely weightless. Like at any given moment I was going to float over the roofs of Loxahatchee and up into the pines. To ground myself, I grabbed an iron skillet and stood in the kitchen, holding it tight with both hands.

19

I NEEDED MONEY. NOT A job: money.

I signed up for OJT (On the Job Training) at school. I'd earn credit for working during the school year, plus I'd learn skills for succeeding in the workforce. I nailed my interview at Dillard's. As an incoming sales associate, I'd be paid minimum wage. "Thank you," I said. "I'm excited!"

I didn't wear my name tag. I pretended to not quite get the cash register. I familiarized myself with the merchandise. Roaming around, I picked out designer clothes for a make-believe rich customer in the dressing room. I folded the clothes into a shopping bag—as though the phantom customer had purchased them—and tossed in a random receipt. I then stashed the bag on the floor inside the most cluttered, un-shoppable clearance rack I could find. When the eyes watching the surveillance cameras switched at shift change, I clocked out for lunch. With nothing unusual about my walk or demeanor, I passed the clearance rack where I'd left the bag. If it was still there—and it always was, no one ever nicked my stash—I faked concern for the cameras—*Oh no!*—and grabbed the bag. Walking through Dillard's, I pretended to look for the fake rich customer who must've set down her bag and forgotten it while shopping. I kept up the act of concerned salesgirl doing good all through the mall, food court, and right to the trunk of my car. After clocking out at the end of my shift, I exited through the loading dock, where Security checked my purse to make sure I hadn't stolen anything. This was protocol. As they must've mentioned twenty times on training day: employee theft costs American companies thirty billion per year.

At home, I admired my stolen goods. I smelled them, folded them, and kept just a few items for myself. New jeans felt so fresh on my skin. I requested Sundays off, "for church."

The air at the Lake Worth Flea Market smelled like turpentine. Everyone was selling stolen stuff: copper wiring, heartburn medication, pharmaceuticals from Mexico. One guy I noticed from the mall. He worked at Payless. Sitting on a soiled mattress, in front of everybody, he chewed the anti-theft devices off the shoes and spit them, full of teeth marks, into a shoebox. The drug-addict vendors were easy to spot. They sold their stuff dirt cheap. I removed chips of brown glass from my little space, which cost me eight bucks. No shade; I spread out my parents' comforter and set the clothes on top. It's laughable now, but I recall being nervous that my parents would get mad at me if they found out I used their comforter in this way.

Big Spanish families, couples with handicapped kids, and girls I hadn't seen since they got pregnant in middle school passed by. "Student discount! Incentives!" I yelled. They rummaged through my boutique of Body Glove bathing suits, Calvin Klein thigh-high socks, Wonderbras, Guess jeans and Guess jean jackets. Sealed bottles of Elizabeth Arden Sunflowers, Joop!, Drakkar Noir, Liz Claiborne Realities, even half-full testers of Tommy Girl I let go for five bucks. I kept a running list of everything I stole and how much I got for each item. Every Sunday, just before bed, I reviewed it. The list was enough to scare me, but not enough to stop me.

Part of OJT was learning about personal finance. Suze Orman's *The 9 Steps to Financial Freedom* was required reading. I loved how Suze used stories of everyday people who faced financial ruin to help guide others away from similar disasters. Her chapter titles resonated with me. They were called "steps," not "chapters": "Step 3: Being Honest with Yourself." "Step 4: Being Responsible to Those You Love." Her feathery hair, her author photo with her dog, the fact that she had worked as a waitress—Suze was a nice lady who would teach me useful shit. All I had to do was follow her program, which involved a little self-discipline and very tiny steps, and I could move forward in life. Once a week, on the porch, I had "Money Night." With a whiskey, a Glade candle, and my back to the pool so I wouldn't get depressed that it was green, I went through the bills—prioritizing utilities, just like Suze recommended. Slipping in the money orders, addressing the envelopes, and licking the stamps gave me a sense of control. Feeling competent (it's such a high to pay the bills when you have money) and a little buzzed from the alcohol, I read Suze's thoughts on ways to maximize one's income.

In the evenings, or after a thunderstorm, when I was sure the migrant pickers had left for the day, I sneaked into Anthony's Groves. The charged air and sweet citrusy fragrance energized me. Far back from the road so no one would see me, down rows of wide, low-hanging trees, I picked navel oranges: bright, firm, and heavy. Even the small ones had the weight of a softball. I tossed them into a pillowcase.

At home, I dug into the very back of my closet. In an old car-battery case decorated with Garbage Pail Kids stickers, I found the syringes I had taken from Lorraine's duplex. I kneaded the oranges on the kitchen tile to soften the flesh. I poured gin into a coffee cup, drew it up into a needle, and injected it into the oranges. At first, I injected fast, like a dart. But then I noticed that shaved-off shards of metal were getting lodged in the pulp. I learned that if I did it slower the needles stayed sharp and lasted longer. I fell asleep naked on top of my sheets, the smell of oranges lingering in my pillowcase. Head buzzing with hope, I waited for the rotating fan to twist in my direction, and for a Friday-night home football game to roll around.

In the school parking lot, under a flood of stars, it was chaos, with everybody descending from the heights of their F-250s. In a dark patch of the lot, my Mustang fit snugly between massive pickups covered in mud. Concealed from the school police, I called out to the kids who passed by, "Alcoholic oranges. Three dollars each, two for five." A green blur of ten-, twenty-dollar bills in my face. I took the money, pulled loose oranges from the back seat, and tossed them to their buyers. "Next!" By the time the players took the field, their bright white helmets visible in the distance, I was fresh out of oranges. I tossed into a plastic grocery bag the evidence they left behind: thick rinds expertly peeled in a single ribbon, the mark of a true Floridian.

It was Senior Night. The last home game I would ever play. "Machinehead" blared through the speakers. The bleachers were full—standing room only. On the sidelines, the woman from the local news station spoke to a camera. College recruiters with their notepads leaned against the wall.

The players from Palm Beach Lakes walked into the gym looking supremely confident. Stakes were high. Whoever won was going to Districts. Palm Beach Lakes had a better record than us, but we had beaten them weeks before, and I was sure we could do it again. Warming up, I kept glancing at the door. I had a weird feeling that my dad was going to show up.

A cop walked in. Brow wrinkled in concentration, he leaned against the same wall as the recruiters—right next to the woman who I was certain was from the University of Miami. I started to think he was there to arrest me for stealing from Dillard's. I tried not to look at him.

In my head, I played out different scenarios. If he arrested me in front of everyone in that gym—college recruiters included—I had to keep my cool. I'd smile. That was my plan: to smile. I felt like I should come up with another one.

I shook my finger. I squeezed it between my thighs. "My finger hurts," I said to my teammate.

"Tape it," she said.

Do it. Now. Fake the injury and go to the locker room. He might follow you and arrest you, but at least it won't be in front of everyone. I couldn't bring myself to do it. I massaged my calves. I took three-pointers from the corner. Every time I wanted to look at the cop, I tightened my ponytail. We gathered at mid-court for tip-off.

I didn't score during the first half—a terrible omen that made me look awful to the recruiters, although some unexpected sharp shooting from Angie DeMello kept us even at the break. Passing the cop on the way to the locker room, I kept my head down. *This is it,* I thought. *He's going to follow me.* When he didn't, I got even more nervous, convinced he was playing mind games with me.

In the locker room, my coach talked directly to me. Without comprehending a word, I nodded. We stacked our hands: Defense! Walking back into the gym, I was certain I was going to vomit. But the cop was gone. For a minute, I thought he'd run to the concession stand, or maybe he hadn't been there at all. Maybe I had imagined the whole thing.

Palm Beach Lakes opened with a full-court press. As they grew more aggressive and took the lead, I got more confident in my game. I passed at half-court, a give-and-go with my shooting guard, then I let fly for three. Angling my feet forward, I stumbled back and hoped for a foul. The whistle came. The three dropped through the rim. I made my foul shot. Shouts and stomping from the bleachers. It was 59–59 going into the fourth.

With three minutes left, the girl guarding me was out of her mind with frustration. She was yelling in my face, slapping my wrists. I dribbled out of it, and before she could follow, I pulled up for a jumper. They answered, and we were down by two.

Sixteen seconds left in the game, and for some reason, Palm Beach Lakes laid off the press. Inbounding was simple, but it felt like they were playing a trick. "Easy, easy," I heard my coach shout. I dribbled down the court. We were short a player. Where was my center? "Easy!" I crossed half-court.

Three of their players circled me. Their hands flew in my face. I picked up my dribble. Squirming away from the heat, I twisted, and faced our defensive basket. That's when I saw my center, Missy Longoria. She was walking up the court— *walking!*—with her hands on her hips. "Come on!" I yelled. Missy stretched out her arms. "Here!" she said. I couldn't throw it to her; it would be a back-court violation. "Come on!" I said again, hands all over me. "I'm right here!" Missy said. I couldn't find the space to throw the ball off my opponent and out of bounds. I called time out just as the whistle blew: five-second rule.

The girls guarding me screamed and jumped into one another's arms. The ref extended his hand for the ball. "I called time out," I said. He shook his head and motioned again for the ball. There was one second left in the game.

I turned around. Missy walked toward me. "I was open," she said.

I swung the ball back as though it were a discus. With all my might, I threw it right off her face. I couldn't believe how far the ball sailed into the bleachers.

Missy went down. I remember people running to her. I made it a point not to look at her. I didn't want to see how bad her face was. Everyone in the bleachers was standing up.

The cheerleaders looked at one another. The lights seemed to get brighter.

The ref grabbed me hard by the arm. "Take her," he yelled. My coach walked at me fast, a wild expression of fury on his face. "Call 911" came from somewhere.

Oh, come on. Nobody needs to call 911.

I don't remember if I just thought that or said it out loud.

20.

IN A SMALL, WINDOWLESS ROOM in a part of the school I'd never seen before, I sat, handcuffed to a chair. The school police officer went through my backpack. She tossed onto the table tests marked with F's, dead lottery tickets, stray Dillard's receipts, orange rinds, and loose, unwrapped tampons speckled with dirt. Principal Hovis stood over me in her Velcro sneakers and hot-pink muumuu. "You defiled the community last night," she said.

I didn't know what "defiled" meant. It sounded like something child molesters did, which made my face get even hotter.

Across from me, on a small couch, sat Missy Longoria. She was wearing a clear plastic face mask just like A. C. Green. Her parents, engrossed in their daughter's pain, smoothed

Missy's hair out of her eyes. They rubbed her back. It was so tender. For the first time, I sensed what it would mean to have caring, responsible parents. No wonder Missy felt comfortable strolling up the court with seconds left on the clock. Her life stakes were low. She could go an entire season without scoring a point; she could go to college, suffer a nervous breakdown, and move back home for the rest of her life. It didn't matter. She'd still be loved. Good parents are bad parents, I thought. I made myself say I was sorry.

"I don't think 'sorry' is enough here, C.C.," Mr. Longoria said.

"No?" I said.

Seconds rolled on in silence. I looked to my coach. Leaning against the wall, arms crossed, he made his eyebrows shoot up. I didn't know what that meant.

"You can sue if you want," I said. Giving people the impression that nothing mattered had become my specialty.

Missy's mom was flabbergasted. I remember her looking around in her red glasses, saying, "In what world? In what world?" It wasn't clear what she was asking. Missy spoke up, but none of us could understand her muffled voice through the mask.

I was thrown off the basketball team and sentenced to four months' In School Suspension (ISS). Six hours a day, five days a week, I sat in the dark auditorium, surrounded by heavy gray curtains and a bunch of other hostile kids. We had to remain in our seats at all times, and anything you can imagine doing while sitting—sleeping, eating, drinking, talking, combing your hair, chewing your nails—was strictly forbidden. If we needed to use the restroom, we had to be escorted. We weren't allowed to go to the cafeteria or the library; the cafeteria and the library had to come to us. Every morning, the ISS teacher, a woman named Citadel who had a military crew cut, wheeled in two carts: one stacked with our coursework, the other with books. On the top two shelves were biographies of rich people. The Kennedys, mostly, but also the Vanderbilts, Henry Flagler, and Marie Antoinette. These books smelled like mold, and I felt flat and dumb while reading them. On the bottom two shelves were criminal memoirs: *My Story* by Amy Fisher, *Pimp: The Story of My Life* by Iceberg Slim. The authors didn't either defend or condemn their behavior. They just shared. What worked, what didn't.

Columbine happened. Every news channel showed the black-and-white surveillance footage of the shooters. Proceeding through the cafeteria, looking aimless, gun in hand, they reminded me of my mother walking around with the shotgun. We got more school police. All the weird kids in ISS started wearing trench coats, because it made them feel powerful. The other kids, who had never even acknowledged the weird kids before, began fighting them. Shortly after, Principal Hovis announced that trench coats were strictly forbidden. Our room—the auditorium—had no windows, and was deemed the safest in the school.

Administration left numerous messages for my parents. I erased them from the answering machine. I received paperwork for my parents to sign. By this point, they had been so uninvolved for so long that my forgery was the authentic signature. No more practice, games, recruitment letters, or OJT, I drove home at three-fifteen. Turning the corner to my street, I anticipated the padlock on the door, and Snickers inside, alone and hungry. I checked to make sure the tire iron

was in my trunk just in case I had to bash a window. I filled
the bathtub with a little bit of hot water and sat in it cross-
legged for hours, wishing I could go back in time. When I
came across basketball games while flipping through channels, I skipped past them fast. The sound of sneakers squeak-
ing on a court was particularly unbearable.

Shame was my go-to emotion. When people talked to or
looked at me, I imagined them saying to themselves, "Now,
there's someone who has a lot of problems." My school
started a recycling program. I passed garbage cans labeled
NORMAL GARBAGE and thought, *That's me.* I felt like the universe had made a collective decision that I was more trouble
than I was worth, and I knew the universe was right. Not like
in a self-pitying way, more just matter-of-fact. I quit shoplift-
ing and stealing from the orange grove. I knew that if I got
caught and went to jail, no one would bail me out.

By the end of the year, I had spent so much time in suspension, and was so oblivious to what my grades were, that I
didn't know if I was going to graduate. "Are they gonna let
you walk?" was the main question of the seniors in ISS, and
none of us had an answer. Citadel said the only way to find
out was to go to the graduation practice and see if our name
was called. On the scheduled day, she escorted us through the
turnstile and into the gym.

We were the last to arrive. The bleachers were packed with
fifteen hundred screaming kids. Citadel lined us up, backs to
the wall. I took in the chaos. The gym seemed so much smaller
than I remembered. Not just small, puny. *This is one shitty
little gym,* I thought.

The cheerleaders ran in hopping, clapping. "OOOeee! It's
hot in here! There must be a Fighting Orange in the atmo-

sphere!" Cartwheels, flips. The kids in the bleachers went crazy. Principal Hovis spoke into a mic, something about how good it felt to look out onto a crowd of clear-eyed, determined young people at the beginning of their adult lives.

The shrill rat-a-tat of the drum corps's snare drums started up and I felt woozy. I didn't want to have to wait for my name. I didn't want to *not* hear it. And if it was said, I didn't want the audience to hear it. I got Citadel's attention. "I'm starting to feel upset," I said.

She walked me over to the emergency exit. "Get some fresh air. But don't go anywhere. Stay right here."

I stepped out directly onto the racquetball court. White-hot sunlight bounced off the thirty-foot-high cement. I remember how good it felt to run to my car.

Two weeks later, I was sitting at the kitchen counter, eating ninety-nine-cent KFC mashed potatoes and looking for jobs in *The Palm Beach Post*'s classifieds. On the last page, there was an ad for an upcoming police auction. Beneath it were two pictures of the 'Vette. One facing the camera, and one in profile, just like a suspect in a lineup.

On the morning of the auction, I drove to the impound lot on the outskirts of Palm Beach County. More cars than buyers beneath a cloudless sky. I walked the yard. Cats prowled in the overgrown grass. Serious-looking men inspected panels and bumper covers, deciphering their scrap value. A spare tire propped up the driver's seat of an old Dodge Dakota. A Mercedes 300D's peeled-up roof revealed an enormous bloodstain on the headrest. From its antenna hung a biohazard tag.

The 'Vette stood apart. Boxed in by cars on every side, it

was the only one that shined. In broad daylight, it seemed tragic that something of such beauty would end up here. Like those pictures you see of dead lions spread before big-game hunters.

I tried the door. It was open. I slid into the driver's seat. The interior was spotless. Stroking its dashboard, I telepathically told it how many great memories it had given us. I thanked it for being so good to my family.

The auctioneer conducted the bidding at tongue-twisting speed from an old green school bus. After selling one car, he cranked up the bus's rough-running engine, nursed it a few feet, and auctioned off the next car. When it was the 'Vette's turn, a woman yelled, "Woooo-eee!" The bidding started at $9,850, and I hoped that my father wasn't here to see that. He'd be devastated.

An elaborate riff of nods and numbers unfolded and shifted so quickly I had a hard time keeping up. A woman with bleached pigtails cranked up the price to $11,000. A man in pleated pants and a button-down—a car salesman, I could tell—offered $11,500.

Pigtails struck back with $11,900. Pleated Pants, $12,200. There were lulls and whispers: "She's done. She don't have it." The auctioneer started talking directly to the bidders, gesturing to them as he urged them on. After a bit of indecision, Pigtails offered $12,900. Pleated Pants didn't hesitate to pop up his number. "Thirteen five. Going once, going twice . . ."

No claps, no cheers. Pleated Pants headed to the office as though he did this every day, which he probably did. The auctioneer moved on to the next in line: a 1987 Honda Spree scooter. Starting bid: thirty-five dollars.

I walked over to the finance trailer, where Pleated Pants was signing documents. I set the title in front of him.

"My dad was a car dealer. I used to go to auctions with him and stand there all day, buying cars." At the memory of my dad's being young and good at his job, my voice broke. "But not like this. Not like motherfuckers like yourself are doing here, at a police auction, with the owner present, holding a title." My tears came fast. I wiped one away, and another one fell.

He narrowed his eyes. He took in my tank top, my jean shorts, my flip-flops.

"How old are you?" he said.

"How old are you?" I set down the keys. "These, and the title. Five hundred bucks."

He reached for his wallet. He unpeeled five one-hundred-dollar bills from the sleeve and handed them to me along with his card: "Al Ciofarri. Trainer, Stapleton Chrysler Dodge." "I hold a seminar once a month for new car salesmen. I'd like you to come."

The seminar, which Al designed himself, was called Good Head: Six and a Half Inches Between the Ears. It took place in a big white conference room at the Dodge dealership off Blue Heron Boulevard. I took a seat at one of the round tables. In front of me was a blank construction-paper nameplate and a Sharpie. "C.C.," I wrote.

The room filled up with about sixty men of all ages, moods, and waistlines. Heavy smokers, I could smell. Each time a new guy sat at my table, he tried to talk to me. Pretending to be busy, I doodled palm trees onto my nameplate. I turned the periods in my name into stars.

Al Ciofarri strolled in, shoulders rolled forward, hands clasped behind his back. "Good head, what is it?" he said to the floor. There was laughter. Al waited for it to die down.

"Right now, your most important goal is your bank account, right? If you had one thousand dollars in your bank account, how would that make you feel?"

Sporadic claps, whistles.

"You'd feel pretty good, right? It's nice to have a little cushion, right? Well, the only way to get there is good head."

Al strolled around the conference room. "Every morning, before I get out of bed, I give myself good head. Every single morning, I say thank you. I can see outside, thank you. I can get up and go to the bathroom on my own, thank you. I have a job, thank you. I have a car, thank you. I have a— Hold on. Before I forget. Everybody's going to pass a drug test, right?"

Murmurs. No laughter.

"What about criminal records? Any felons here? Registered felons in the room?"

Some hands went up. Al counted them. "Two, three, six. Okay, come see me on our break." He continued to stroll.

"It's not a coincidence that you're here. I handpicked each and every one of you. You're here because, the minute I saw you, in your circumstances, I knew exactly what you needed to succeed."

"GOOD HEAD," he wrote on the dry erase board.

"What does 'good head' mean? It means keeping the enemies and the demons out. Good head is controlling the secret language that goes on in the six and a half inches between your ears. 'I can do it,' 'No, I can't'; 'I can do it,' 'No, I can't'; 'I can do it,' 'No, I can't.' You're here because I took one look at you and I knew, immediately: *Yes, you can do it.*

"If you can convince me you can sell cars, I will give you a job. Stapleton is getting ready to open several dealerships across the U.S. We have one openin' in Orlando. One in Asheville. Next year, Westport, Connecticut. That's the Gold Coast, people. Highest median credit score in the nation. Land a job there, you will make more your first year than an aerospace engineer."

Al handed out his specially designed "Professional Automotive Consultants Manual." On the first page was a list of things to never say in a dealership.

> Number one: Can I help you? (They will say no.)
> Number two: Trust me.

On our second day of the seminar, Al had us watch *Rocky*. At the end of the movie, just as Paulie redeemed himself from all the shitty things he'd done by pulling up the rope to let Adrian slip into the ring, Al pushed "stop." I was surprised to hear sniffles. Some of the guys were crying.

"What is this movie about?" Al said.

No one answered.

"Is it about winning? No. Is it about fighting? No. Is it about the price you have to pay to be on top? No. This movie, this *masterpiece*, is about a man's desire to get by in the world without being a bum."

Al flipped on the overhead lights. After a long silence, he said, gravely, "Power on that good head."

We paired up for role play. A guy stepped toward me. He was handsome and built. Sandy blond hair wisped into his blue eyes. I felt my face get warm.

"Like my tie?" he said.

"It's okay."

"Where'd you meet Al?"

"Where'd you meet him?"

"I asked you first."

"I'm not telling you."

"Wendy's," he said.

"Do you work there?"

"No, I don't *work* there. You're beautiful, by the way."

I shut off the lights inside me.

I raised a wall.

"I'll be the salesman," I said. "You be the customer."

On the night before my audition, in the garage's fluorescent white light, I practiced the walk-around on my Mustang and pretend customers. "All right! So I brought you out here. The dealership is just too hectic, too much going on. It's more comfortable beside this . . . lawn mower. Now, what I want is to take you step by step through all the qualities of this gorgeous, third-generation Mustang five-point-oh. When you look at the car, from the front, what is the first thing you see? That's right. The grille. A seven-slotted grille. The seven slots allow for more airflow, keeping the engine cool. When an engine is cool, it doesn't have to work as hard. And by not working hard, it gives better gas mileage."

I popped the hood with one hand.

"Let's take a look at the engine. A five-point-oh Windsor V-eight. Iron block, iron cylinder heads—this is a very charismatic engine. It revs quickly. Total output of two hundred and fifteen horsepower, two hundred and ninety pounds of torque. Here's your radiator. Your intercooler. No. Wait."

Shoot. I took a deep breath. I checked my notes. "Bear with me, please. I'm new."

21.

IN 2013, AT THE BOTTOM of the recession, I found a house I wanted to buy: a two-bedroom, one-bath cottage, built in 1927. Viewing it with the agent, I stood in the Florida room and cranked open the jalousie windows. I looked out to tall coconut palms, swaying in the ocean breeze, and an outdoor shower covered in a mess of pink bougainvillea.

The house cost $127,000, which was in my budget, but the mortgage-loan originator said it was a bad financial idea. The Intracoastal was just two blocks away. At every full moon, water cascaded over the seawall and flooded Flagler Drive. Which is why everyone's lawn was yellow and not green. My insurance rate would skyrocket every year. Ten years from now there was a good chance that insurance wouldn't be offered at all.

"After the closing, you're going to have twenty-six dollars left to your name. You realize that," he said.

"Yeah, but I'm gonna have a house."

After a lifetime of trailers, campgrounds, foreclosures, apartments not in my name, and sublet after sublet, after Craigslist, Airbnb, Vrbo, I had my own spot in the world. Falling asleep on the first night in my new home to the *swoosh-swoosh* of the running dishwasher was one of the happiest moments in my life. I felt grounded, which was weird, considering I was broke and falling asleep on an air mattress.

At work, I created the program for our annual gala—our biggest night of the year. It sounds easy, but there was real strategy involved. To secure interviews with our biggest donors, I created a customized "persuasion" card that invited participation. It included a response telephone number (which had to be a landline), promises of future contact, a copy of last year's glossy gala program, and a list of reasons for participating ("give a voice to our animals"). The envelope, decorated with a dignified Florida Zoo logo, had to be postage-stamped, not metered. All of this was time-consuming and expensive, and the only way the super-wealthy would respond.

They all lived on Palm Beach Island, in old-money estates along Ocean Boulevard. It was a little nerve-racking to approach their long, manicured drives and come up to the gates of the properties, which had to be opened manually.

"You've led a very interesting life!" I said, feeling scratchy in my wool Chanel minidress, black with white trimming. I'd bought it at a consignment shop on Dixie Highway. It was my "economic success" outfit. The donors invited me to join them in their parlors. I felt emotional connections with their wallpaper. Fields of plump red tulips, and hydrangeas sprouting vaginas. A motif of vipers wrapped around bamboo, embedded with strips of mother-of-pearl. At one estate, I found myself gawking at a wash of smoky charcoal blasted by a spray of gold, resembling stars in the night sky. The donor finally explained: "It's hand-painted."

They were all women, old, very thin women with odd accents. "World English," I later learned, but, encountering it for the first time, I assumed they had suffered strokes.

"So, Mrs. Cromwell. Can you tell me a little bit about your relationship to animals?" I said, tapping "record" on my phone.

"We had a ranch in Montana, the estate did. For my thirteenth birthday, I received my own bison herd. They ran through everything. They were very strong. I helped to breed them and raise them. They were very bad-tempered. Like any wild animals when they feel threatened."

"Thank you for meeting with me, Mrs. Chambers. I know you have given so much to the zoo, and I'm curious. Can you tell me about your favorite experience with an animal?"

"Of course. It was in the Maasai Mara. A reliable African told me that a black rhinoceros had given birth. Well, of course, I outfitted my Land Cruiser and headed for the river!"

I swallowed my tea biscuit. "Wait. Mrs. Koch. I'm sorry. I think I missed something. This was the rarest bird in the world, and you saw it twice?"

"Yes, dear. Once in Murchison Falls in Uganda. Then again, years later, in Lake Manyara in Tanzania. I took twelve days to go down the river, birding all the way . . ."

I drove through an acre of mangrove and cabbage palms. On a balcony, beneath a carved stone arch, I met with our biggest donor.

Renee Cutter's hobby was wildlife photography. She showed me her darkroom. In several pans of acid, we watched prints come to life. Black-and-white portraits of female leopards denning in a gorge, their babies hidden among rocks. "People think pictures of leopards in trees are exciting, but that's only because it's exciting just to see a leopard," she said. "It doesn't, to my eye, have half the intrigue of seeing one in a den, in an area in which they live. To glimpse a leopard mother with her babies—how she copes and adjusts—that's what reveals the mysteries of nature."

I examined the photograph that we'd be putting on the cover of the gala program: a mother leopard lying languorously beside her two cubs, damselflies swarming over their heads.

"How close were you to them?" I said.

"Thirty feet. I was in my Land Cruiser. You don't get out of your vehicle with an animal like that. When you're in their world, you must be mindful of distance and position. You don't want to interfere with their life in any way. Always stay downwind, not upwind. That way your scent won't send them away."

The gala sold out—$575 a head, invite only—and the Mar-a-Lago Grand Ballroom was packed. Crystal chandeliers the size of VW Bugs hung from the gold-plated ceiling. Guests arrived in floor-length dresses with sparkling evening bags. They kissed one another's cheeks. They posed for pictures on the marble staircase. I kept peeking out from behind the gold curtain, where I huddled with my boss, Mr. Chase. He went over the latest draft of the speech that I'd written for him, one last time.

"'Dear friends, blah blah blah. . . . It is most appreciated . . . blah blah blah.'" He rolled his neck. "'W. C. Barron, the founder of Wall Street's *Barron's,* said early in this century that the only values in the state of Florida are the values created by man. This was how the state was perceived by the wealthy who came from elsewhere to exploit it.'"

He shot me a look.

"What? I got that from my favorite Key West guidebook. I left out the names of the families who did the early exploiting, like you said."

He continued reading: "'Florida, our eccentric, scruffy state, was once a wild tropical paradise—a place people and animals flocked to when they were threatened out of their own territory. But decades of mistreatment have taken their toll. More than half of the Everglades is now farms and cities; the groundwater is brackish. It is unclear how its animals and its people will adapt to the destruction. Or whether they will at all.'

"'Everglades' is in the verbiage guide, C.C. The lawyers for Big Sugar are in attendance tonight."

"Sorry."

He crossed out the whole paragraph. "'This year's gala theme—"Nocturnal Jungle"—is a wonderful choice. We are recognizing the cup of night, which is naturally associated with vulnerability.' "

He looked up. " 'Cup of night,' " he muttered.

"Play on words. Tarot-related," I said.

" '. . . Night brings a pressure of feeling. It also offers up inspiration. Soon after Van Gogh admitted himself to the asylum, he wrote to his brother, "I . . . need a starry night." It was at night that Muhammad made his journey from Mecca to Jerusalem and then to heaven. In Jewish tradition, the beginning of a new day is at nightfall. We begin again, with night.' "

He crossed out everything after "starry night."

"That's the artistic part," I said.

"These are women who lunch, C.C. They don't have any interest in hearing about Muhammad."

"That's not true. They're worldly."

" 'Proceeds, blah blah blah, will help the zoo advance its mission: to offer animals a place to be alive.' "

He mulled it over. "You think that's enough? For our mission statement?" he said.

"Yeah."

He looked skeptical. "I'd like to think that we offer them a little more than a place to live. I'm sure the donors would."

"What do you mean? People spend their entire lives looking for that."

Immediately following Lorraine's release from prison, I drove her to Florida and moved her into a sober-living house. Debbie D's cost $205 a week out of pocket, and the rest was covered by insurance. If Lorraine stayed sober, Debbie D's was perfect. And even if she relapsed, which I was certain she would do, and probably several times, it was still perfect. Debbie D assured me that Debbie D's was the best place in Florida to be an addict—recovering or active. There was a Publix in walking distance. Its pharmacy sold syringes without a prescription. Suboxone was sold on the street. She also made it clear that she was open to gaming insurance rules. "If need be, my clients travel Blue Cross Country," she said. Meaning: if Lorraine's insurance money dried up, she could use again, which would force her insurance into covering her again, and Debbie D would help her find a different facility that would take her in. This is total fraud, and costs insurance companies millions of dollars, but it's also the only way for addicts to avoid ending up on the streets. I helped Lorraine open a bank account, buy a flip phone, and apply for disability. I gave her a long hug goodbye.

Debbie D's Sober Living had a pool, and little concrete tables shaded by blue-and-pink umbrellas. Once in a while, I'd drive by and see Lorraine smoking beneath them, drinking Red Bull, talking and sometimes laughing with the other people who lived there. I didn't tell Lorraine that I lived in Florida, just twenty minutes from Debbie D's. I kept my Connecticut license plate and cell number as a form of protection—just like a bulletproof vest.

In my contacts, I saved Lorraine as "Mentally Ill Sister." When she called, hysterical, or asking for money, that description appeared, reminding me that the person I was about to speak to was vulnerable, but also compromised, and that no amount of money or reasoning or urgency on my part would make that go away. Sometimes, my withholding of where I lived made me feel deceitful, but it was the boundary I set. She could count on me for care and guidance, but little else. Plus, it wasn't like I actively lied to Lorraine. She never asked where I lived.

On holidays, I did surprise drop-ins. We'd attend her NA meeting, then go back to her little room. Listening to Linkin Park on low volume, I helped her with her outpatient-program homework. I asked and she answered the worksheet questions:

How justified was your paranoia today?
What did you dream of last night?
What kind of bad things float through your head if you don't control it?

My father was harder to keep an eye on. He migrated from town to town, shelter to shelter. When he wanted to drink, he drank, which is why he was always getting kicked out. I drove by his dwellings; I scanned the sidewalks. It was rare to find him asleep, but when I did, I set by his side some bananas, water, and expensive medical-grade sunblock. Just like Mrs. Wellman said: you don't want too much exposure to the elements. Sometimes, I'd go back to my car and watch, to make sure nothing attacked him. Other times, I woke him up. "Pumpkin! How you always find me?" he'd say. But it was hyperbole; he didn't wait for an answer.

Recently, he somehow acquired a car: a Buick Roadmaster, same make and model that Grandpa Borkoski drove. He nicknamed it "The Hotel" and moved into the parking lot of the Immokalee Indian Reservation. He wakes up at two, three in the morning, goes into the casino, and plays the penny slots.

Last Thanksgiving, I visited him. I rapped on his window and waved. We walked to the casino for dinner. The parking lot was the size of a football field, and there was no shade. Row after row, I noticed other people living in their cars. Windows down, a man smoked in his underwear. A couple climbed over seats, searching for something, bickering. A woman breastfed a baby, her long black hair piled under its body, supporting it like a nest. They sat beside baseball bats, Igloo coolers, laundry baskets filled with deodorant, diapers, the kind of toys you win from the claw machine. I saw a gray, panting pit bull and a cardboard sign on the dashboard, "My Dog Eats First." I heard ghostlike coughs and sniffs of nasal spray. They ate potato chips, they listened to music, they stared into space. My father pointed them out. "See, kid? They're just like me."

Around the corner from my house, a power plant runs along a lagoon. A metropolis of humming engines, fire pumps, generators, and storage tanks that hold millions of gallons of fuel oil. It's a paradise for wildlife. Environmentalists and activists get so happy when power plants close, but the truth is, turtles, sharks, stingrays, and especially manatees (who are an endangered species and can't survive in water that dips below sixty-eight degrees) depend on power plants. The ocean in Florida gets too cold for them, and all their usual wintering spots have been destroyed. The power plants have all closed in Northern and Central Florida, so this one is all they have left. If something happens to it, there's no way South Florida will be able to sustain such a large influx of displaced manatees.

Often, after work, I brown-bag a Miller Lite, walk to the power plant, and sit on the cement seawall. Legs dangling over the clear, shallow water, I can see straight to the sandy bottom. Loggerhead turtles munch on seaweed. Hammerhead sharks dart back and forth to move forward. Manatees swim so close to me I can see their bristly muzzles, deep-set eyes, and innocent expressions.

Dozens of them congregate near the plant's basin. In the sun's gold glitter, they play in the warm-water discharge.

ACKNOWLEDGMENTS

In the years (and years) it took me to write this book, I have relied on many people for all kinds of things. Robert Anasi, Brendan Beirne, Andrew Blauner, Ryan Carrasco, Alan Denkenson, DV DeVincentis, Rob Ehle, Jack Fox, Jamie Fox, Carolina Freitas da Cunha, Dr. G, Peter Gethers, Lee and Sandi Greco, Kehlila Green-Moore, Laura Harrison, Tim and Loring Hart-Woods, Cliff Hertz, Ratt Ito, Leslie Jaworski, Alicia Oltuski, James Repici, Erik Seidel, Jeremy and Jocelyn Smerd, Katharine Smyth, Tatiana Kushnarenko, David Vigliano, David Williams—each of you, at some point (or many points), took time away from your lives to help me with mine. I am eternally grateful and indebted.

To the editors I've had along the way: Julie Grau, Susan

Kamil, and Robin Desser—your faith, knowledge, and expertise helped me grow as a person and as a writer. I am particularly grateful to my editor, Andrea Walker, who showed up for me in all the ways I desperately needed. I'm proud of this book because of you.

I would also like to thank MacDowell, Yaddo, the Kerouac Project of Orlando, and the Florida Division of Cultural Affairs. Your commitment to the arts made it possible for me to meet like-minded fuckups and see this project through.

Finally, to my family. My nephew, Jacob, for sharing and listening and understanding, always. Junior, for being the bottomless barrel of joy that you are. Senior, for going with me on the ultimate journey. My sister, the original badass truth teller, who screamed it from the rooftops. And my father, who died while I was writing this book. I love you and thank you for your tolerance as I rummaged through the debris.

ABOUT THE AUTHOR

BETH RAYMER is the author of *Lay the Favorite*, a memoir about her years in Las Vegas and her work in the sports-betting industry, which was made into a feature film directed by Stephen Frears and starring Rebecca Hall and Bruce Willis. She received an M.F.A. from Columbia University and was awarded a Fulbright scholarship. Her journalism has been published in *The Atlantic* and *The New York Times Magazine*. This is her first novel.

ABOUT THE TYPE

This book was set in Sabon, a typeface designed by the well-known German typographer Jan Tschichold (1902–74). Sabon's design is based upon the original letter forms of sixteenth-century French type designer Claude Garamond and was created specifically to be used for three sources: foundry type for hand composition, Linotype, and Monotype. Tschichold named his typeface for the famous Frankfurt typefounder Jacques Sabon (c. 1520–80).